"I'll chance it," Scott replied, steering around a corner.

"What's next, a duel?" she demanded. "Pistols at ten paces?"

"Sorry, you're out of luck—I'm abducting you, remember? We're going to my apartment."

"And just why am I going to your apartment?"

"Dinner. And a discussion."

She crossed her arms. "I have nothing to say to you. I've had enough." Matrice reached for the door handle. The car swerved as Scott pulled her hand away, then steered into his parking space.

"No, you haven't—you've only had half. We both have. It's about time that stopped."

"I'll get a cab," she announced, getting out and slamming the door in her wake. She took two steps before Scott picked her up and threw her over his shoulder, fireman-style. "Put me down, Scott! What are you doing?"

Scott began walking to the elevator. "Friday is taking Ms. Crusoe home with him...."

Dear Reader,

Summer may be over, but autumn has its own special pleasures—the bright fall foliage and crisp, starry nights. It's the perfect time to curl up with a Silhouette Romance novel.

This month, we continue our FABULOUS FATHERS series with Nick Elliot, the handsome hero of Carla Cassidy's *Pixie Dust.* Under the influence of a little girl's charms and a mother's beauty, even a sworn bachelor can become enchanted by family life.

Love and miracles are alive and well in Duncan, Oklahoma! This little town with a lot of heart is the setting for Arlene James's brand new trilogy, THIS SIDE OF HEAVEN. The series starts off this month with *The Perfect Wedding*—a heartwarming lesson in the healing power of love.

In Elizabeth Krueger's *Dark Prince,* Celia Morawski accepts Jared Dalton's marriage proposal while tangled in the web of her own lies. But is it possible her prince has secrets darker than her own?

Be sure not to miss the fiery words and sizzling passion as rivals fall in love in Marie Ferrarella's *Her Man Friday.* Look for love and laughter in Gayle Kaye's *His Delicate Condition.* And new author Liz Ireland has lots of surprises in store for her heroine—and her readers—in *Man Trap.*

In the months to come, look for more books from some of your favorite authors, including Diana Palmer, Elizabeth August, Suzanne Carey and many more.

Until then, happy reading!

Anne Canadeo
Senior Editor
Silhouette Books

HER MAN FRIDAY
Marie Ferrarella

Silhouette
ROMANCE™
Published by Silhouette Books New York
America's Publisher of Contemporary Romance

To Charlie, who is still my first choice to be
marooned with and who is living proof that complete
opposites *do* attract and can stay that way

SILHOUETTE BOOKS
300 East 42nd St., New York, N.Y. 10017

HER MAN FRIDAY

Copyright © 1993 by Marie Rydzynski-Ferrarella

All rights reserved. Except for use in any review, the reproduction
or utilization of this work in whole or in part in any form by any
electronic, mechanical or other means, now known or hereafter
invented, including xerography, photocopying and recording, or in
any information storage or retrieval system, is forbidden without
the permission of the publisher, Silhouette Books, 300 E. 42nd St.,
New York, N.Y. 10017

ISBN: 0-373-08959-7

First Silhouette Books printing September 1993

Printed in the U.S.A.

MARIE FERRARELLA

was born in Europe, raised in New York City and now lives in Southern California. She describes herself as the tired mother of two overenergetic children and the contented wife of one wonderful man. She is thrilled to be following her dream of writing full-time.

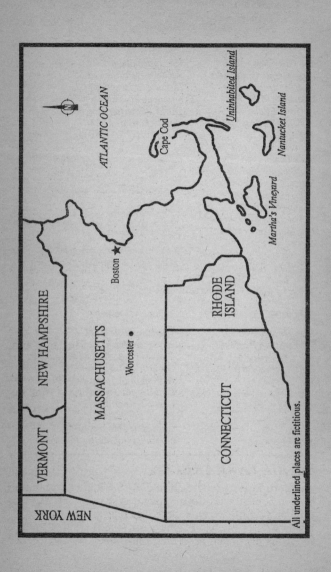

VERMONT

NEW HAMPSHIRE

NEW YORK

MASSACHUSETTS

Worcester •

★ Boston

CONNECTICUT

RHODE ISLAND

ATLANTIC OCEAN

Cape Cod

Uninhabited Island

Nantucket Island

Martha's Vineyard

All underlined places are fictitious.

Chapter One

For Scott diMarco, it all began as a misunderstanding. A carelessly thrown-out line in the midst of a conversation with his sister-in-law; it had had absolutely no conscious thought behind it.

"What you need, Scottie, is for someone to find you a wife. One with tastes and a background similar to yours. You know, the way they used to do in the old country," Valerie diMarco said to him as she cleared away the dessert plates. She'd used the delicate china with the light pink design, the set she favored when the meal really meant something special. The way it did whenever Scott came to Sunday brunch.

She gave a smart shake of her head to emphasize her statement. Valerie and Scott's brother, Frank, had taken him in at the age of twelve, when his parents had died and he had found his secure world suddenly shattered. She was fifty percent sister-in-law, fifty percent mother and one hundred percent friend to him. Which was why he allowed her to lecture him at times like this. He knew she always meant well.

Out of affection, Scott let her expound for a few minutes on the subject of why he needed a wife. He had to admit that she had a lot of excellent, logical points. His brother merely sat back, nursing his last cup of coffee, and tuned her out the way spouses did when well-worn topics came up. Scott didn't tune Valerie out. He never did. She talked, he listened. He owed her that and a great deal more.

He was different around her, Frank and his two nephews than he was in his workaday world. He could relax here, be himself. In some ways, this was more home to him than his own apartment. His own apartment reflected one aspect of his life: Scott, the successful stockbroker. This apartment represented a lot of warm memories. And a feeling of security he was never really able to generate for himself on his own.

When Valerie finally came up for air, Scott quickly took his opportunity. "Fine," he said fondly, kissing the top of her head as he slipped on his jacket. "You find me one. You have the specs."

Valerie stopped folding linen napkins and looked at him. "You're serious?"

"About the wife?" Yes, he thought. Maybe he was at that. Maybe it was time.

A faraway look took hold of Valerie's face. Her mind began to race ahead a mile a minute as she plotted. "No, about the specs."

What was she up to? he wondered. He knew her well enough to recognize the signs. Scott paused, considering her question. "Yes. If I were to look for a wife, which I haven't the time for," he added quickly, seeing the bright light that was growing in her eyes, "she'd have to be compatible with my way of life, just as you mentioned. Same background, same education, same goals, you know. A female version of me.''

"A female Scott diMarco." Frank laughed as he rose from the table. "Now there's a gruesome thought." Placing one hand comfortably on Valerie's shoulder, he followed his younger brother to the front door.

Scott never left a challenge unanswered, even one raised in jest. "No, actually, it's a logical thought, now that Val's raised it. Half the people I know who got married after bumping into one another in a lodge at Vail or one of those trendy 'in' places are getting a divorce citing 'irreconcilable differences.'" A disparaging smile flitted across his lips. "They *thought* they knew what they were getting when they waltzed up the aisle. The simple fact was that they didn't. They knew one, maybe two facts, let physical attraction take over and wham, the surprise package they rushed home with exploded on them. I want no surprises.''

Frank shook his head. He was a romantic through and through and proud of it. It was in his genes, in his heritage. He had always assumed Scott was the same. Obviously not. "Where's the romance, Scottie?"

"Under *R* in the dictionary." There were a lot more important things to consider than burning with passion for someone, Scott thought. Like compatibility.

Frank slapped Scott on the back. "Where have I gone wrong, kid?"

Too busy planning, Valerie failed to notice the disappointed tone in her husband's voice. "Should she be pretty?"

She was really getting into this, wasn't she, Scott thought with a grin. He shrugged. "It wouldn't hurt, but no, it doesn't matter that much.''

"As long as she doesn't scare away small dogs and children,'' Frank interjected.

Scott nodded, playfully clipping Frank on the arm. "Sounds good to me." Giving Valerie a hug, he kissed her goodbye. "You get to work on it, Val, see what you can come up with." It was said to indulge her and with no more seriousness than if he was ordering a corned beef on rye from the corner deli. Less.

He forgot about the conversation as soon as he was in the elevator, traveling the fifteen floors to street level.

And he didn't remember it. Until the following Wednesday, when the phone rang in his office. Wrestling with data he was compiling on his computer, Scott let his telephone ring eight times before he finally picked up the receiver.

"DiMarco," he snapped. A foreign dignitary had almost been assassinated this morning while visiting the Middle East on a goodwill tour and all hell had broken loose. The market, mirroring the world as it always did, had been going crazy all morning.

"It's Val. I did it."

It took him a moment to pull himself together. He made it a policy to keep a very distinct line between his work personality and the one he displayed around his family. "Hi, Val. Sorry I snapped at you. It's been murder around here since I first walked in." Turning his chair away from his view of the rest of the outer office, he searched for an island of peace. "Did what?"

"I found you a wife."

There was a sudden uproar on the floor and he heard the loud reverberations through the thick glass that surrounded his office, but for once he didn't wonder what was rising or falling, beyond his adrenaline. He sat up, fully alert.

"What?" She had to be kidding. Valerie had a very unique sense of humor.

He heard the patient sigh on the other end. She'd used the same tone with him when he had been younger and particularly inattentive. It was as close as Valerie ever came to reprimanding him. This wasn't shaping up to be a joke.

"You told me to, remember? Last Sunday, after brunch," she added when he made no reply. "You said you wanted to marry someone exactly like you, a match the way they used to do back in the days when marriages lasted. Well, I found her, Scottie." Val's voice swelled with excitement. "She's perfect. She fits you like a glove."

He could hear the pleased smile in Valerie's voice. "I wasn't planning on wearing her."

"Not until after you're married." That was the mother in her coming out. All her maternal instincts told Valerie that this was going to be just perfect. She could just feel it. The only thing she wondered about was why it hadn't hit her before. She'd known Rita Crusoe for three years now and had met her daughter on one occasion. But Valerie had never thought of the girl as the perfect mate for Scott until she'd met Rita for lunch on Tuesday and had mentioned her conversation with Scott. After that, the pieces had all fallen together with lightning speed.

Scott knew she had his best interest at heart, but there were times when Valerie did go off the deep end. Like now. "Val, I really—"

She wasn't about to let him get a protest in. This was too good for him to pass up. It was her opinion that he hadn't taken enough time to enjoy any of the fruits of his labors. It was high time he did.

"Scottie, she really is perfect. The same background, the same type of college, career—even genealogy," Valerie rattled off quickly. "You couldn't ask for a better match." She remembered her husband's comment. "And she doesn't have a face that will scare away small dogs and children. In fact, she's very pretty. There's compatibility written all over this."

Scott leaned back in his chair, shutting out the swell of noise outside. It was insane, he knew, but he was beginning to entertain positive feelings about this idea. "And just where did you meet Miss Right?" He knew that Valerie meant well and that she had good instincts. And God knew his schedule was so tight, he didn't have the time to really look around himself. There were a lot of good reasons for having a compatible mate chosen for him by a competent loved one.

"I know her mother, Rita. As a matter of fact, Rita's one of my closest friends. You've heard me talk about her. She's the woman I met at that charity fund-raiser three years ago."

He vaguely remembered. "Oh." The word *competent* was suddenly in jeopardy.

Valerie knew that tone. "Don't 'oh' me, Scottie. I've really studied her background and everything, just as you wanted me to."

He thought it useless to point out that he had just been humoring her at the time. She wouldn't take kindly to that. Valerie didn't like to be humored; she liked to be taken seriously, especially when her heart was in it, as it seemed to be this time.

"This is the best deal you'll ever see, Scott Mario di-Marco, and if you pass it up—"

He knew she could go on like this for a long time, longer than he had. He decided to relent. Besides, if it did turn out the way she claimed, it could be very beneficial to both him and his prospective bride.

Scott shook his head. Married. Him. It had a strange, but not altogether unwelcome ring to it.

"You're absolutely right, Val." He knew that took the wind out of her sails for a moment. "I do need a wife, I just never got around to finding one."

"That's what I'm here for," she answered cheerfully, glad that was over with.

"Okay, set it up for me." He began to rise. The natives outside his door were getting progressively restless and it was time to rejoin the madness. There were commissions to earn and, more important, a reputation to uphold.

"Uh-uh. Some things, Scottie, you have to do for yourself."

He was in this now. He might as well go all the way. Scott pulled over a sheet of paper. "Okay, what's her number?"

Valerie fairly beamed over the telephone. "She works for Atkinson, Mayer and Brown. Her number is—wait, I have it right here."

Valerie recited a number as Scott wrote it down, frowning. Atkinson, Mayer and Brown was his firm's leading competitor. Well, at least she worked for the best. Second best, he amended. "Got it." He tucked the paper under his desk calendar.

"Scott?"

"Yes?"

"You haven't asked her name."

"Oh, right." He pulled back the paper and reached for his pen. "Well, if she's the right one, her name'll be Honey."

"She's the right one, all right. But I'm not too sure if she'd want to be called Honey. Her name is Mary Therese Crusoe. Most people call her Matrice."

He made a note of that, too.

Mary Therese Crusoe was beginning to feel as if her entire adult life had been conducted on automatic pilot. It was the best method, she'd found, to get through the day, doing a score of things that normally required two and a half people, working full-time, to accomplish. She prided herself on her speed and her abilities. If the word *workaholic* was bandied about behind her back, so what? She always got the job done. That had earned her the honor of being the youngest stockbroker ever, never mind female stockbroker, in the firm.

What had been missing in all this was a partner. Matrice was twenty-eight years old and lived alone except for a teacup white poodle that seemed to think the roles of owner and pet were reversed. She hadn't really envisioned herself as being twenty-eight without a husband, an equal at her side to share triumphs and disappointments with. Matrice had never wasted time with daydreams about the perfect knight in the shining armor galloping into her life and sweeping her off her feet. She hadn't wanted to be swept away. She was far too practical for that. But she did want to travel through life's roads with someone other than her poodle, Travis, at her side, his ears flapping in the wind as he hung out the window of her car.

She grinned to herself. That was also an apt description of the last man she had gone out with before she'd thrown up her hands and declared herself out of the rat race for a spouse for good. The declaration had been made that Sunday to her mother several blocks away from where Scott was having brunch with Valerie and Frank.

"I mean it, Mother. You're just going to have to face the fact that you are never going to be a mother-in-law, much less a grandmother, unless, of course, Travis gets some dog in trouble."

Rita Crusoe frowned. It was a soft frown, but it carried weight. She glanced at the dog, resting on the floor in her kitchen. "I never wanted to be a grandmother *that* much." She knew that, after a month of Saturdays spent curled up in front of her TV with a lapful of work, Mary Therese had finally gone out on a date. "Last night not go well?"

Matrice tried to nudge a cherry out of the bottom of her fruit cocktail. "The sinking of the *Titanic* was less of a disaster." Matrice dragged a hand through a turmoil of chestnut-brown hair that insisted on remaining unruly, responding to the humidity in the air. "They say that there are good men out there, but I sure don't know where they're hiding. The only ones I ever seem to run into are the ones that come out of the woodwork when it rains." She secured the cherry and popped it into her mouth, satisfied with the small triumph.

Mrs. Crusoe's delicate eyebrows narrowed. "So you're giving up?"

"Yes," Matrice answered cheerfully. It almost felt good to announce herself out of the running. No more stilted conversations, no more awkward moments at the door. No more multilimbed men to fight off like that last one, Wyatt something-or-other, who was still leaving messages on her answering machine even after a month.

The cheerfulness had a false ring to it. Rita Crusoe would have bet several shares of stock on it. "That doesn't sound like you."

Matrice placed her spoon next to the slender dessert cup. "Mother, I've put in a lot of nerd miles. I've gone out with a fair amount of men and there's always been something lacking in them. Right around the second date, if we got that far, there'd be this sinking sensation in the pit of my stomach and I'd just want to run for the hills." She rose and walked to the terrace. This morning there was a good breeze, although the August day promised to be as stifling hot as the ones that had come before. Matrice looked out. Twenty stories up, the view of New York was magnificent. It always served to calm her.

Her mother's voice followed her as she watched Matrice from the dining room table. "What you need is someone more like you, more centered."

"Maybe." Matrice watched a pigeon try to maneuver against a sudden strong gust and get pushed in the opposite direction. Maybe that was like her, too.

"More attuned to things that you like."

"That would be nice," Matrice murmured vaguely.

Rita Crusoe touched her fingers together lightly, steepling them as she watched Matrice's back. "A man who understands what you have to put up with in your line of work."

Matrice turned around to look at her mother. Fifty-nine and the woman looked at least ten years younger. Her mother probably had more of a chance of getting married again than she did.

"Exactly." Matrice crossed the room and dropped back into her seat. "Seen any of those lying around?" The remark was meant to be teasingly flippant.

Rita didn't take it that way. She was utterly serious. "If I did, would you be interested?"

Matrice traced the delicate pattern on the spoon with her fingertip. It had been her father's last gift to her mother before he died. Kind, considerate, dependable. They just didn't make men like John Crusoe anymore, she mused. "Don't play cagey with me, Mother. Of course I'd be interested."

Rita Crusoe leaned forward, placing a well-manicured hand on her daughter's. There were no rings on Matrice's hands, no polish on her nails. She had always been just a little too utilitarian for her mother's tastes, but Rita had always let her daughter go her own way. Until now. "Then you do want to get married."

"Yes, of course I do," Matrice answered impatiently. It wasn't as if she hadn't been trying. Sort of. "If he has certain qualities."

The thoughtful expression remained on her mother's face. "Just what do you want in a male?"

"Why?" Matrice looked at her mother suspiciously. "Are you going to have Aunt Bianca conjure one up for me?" Aunt Bianca was her father's great-aunt, and the family eccentric, who claimed to dabble in spells and black magic. Every one in the family humored the old woman. When she had been very young, Matrice had honestly believed that Aunt Bianca really could cast spells.

Rita waved her hand at the statement. "Nothing so barbaric. In the old country, they used to call it going through a matchmaker."

Maybe she was overreacting to last night's date from hell. A few months ago, Matrice would have called that method an archaic remnant of the past. But right about now, the idea of a matchmaker, someone who intelligently took everything into consideration when-pairing up two people, sounded pretty good to her. At least, it was worth listening to.

"Just what do you have in mind?"

Her mother smiled the same kind of smile that da Vinci had first captured in the Mona Lisa as she leaned over and patted Matrice's hand just once. A sign of surety. "Mary Therese, you just leave it all to me."

And, because her mother was the most competent, responsible woman she knew, Matrice decided to do just that. Who knew what might come of it?

With life going at a gallop, Matrice didn't give the matter any more thought until her mother called her the following Wednesday at her office.

"It's done."

Her mother didn't believe in opening salutations. "Hello, Mother." Matrice hit two keys simultaneously on the computer and scrolled down to the next screen, searching for the elusive figure that had been playing hide-and-seek with her for the better part of an hour. She pressed the speaker phone key on her multiline system and returned the receiver to the cradle. "What's done?"

Her mother's voice filled the small office. "That little detail of finding you a mate for life. Remember our talk?"

"Vaguely." Matrice stopped scrolling as her mother's words penetrated. Her eyes widened. "A husband? You found me a husband?" Quickly Matrice snatched up the receiver and jabbed the button on her phone system again, returning her mother's voice to the privacy of the telephone receiver. "That was rather fast, wasn't it? Were they having a sale at Neiman Marcus?"

A husband. A cold wave swept over her, which she shook off.

"Don't be flippant, Mary Therese. It doesn't become you. It's just that I have connections."

"In the black market?" She could almost envision her mother placing an order for one upper-class, purebred husband and asking to have him delivered to the penthouse for Sunday brunch.

On her end, Rita thought of Valerie diMarco and smiled. Valerie had told her of her brother-in-law's "plight" over lunch. Talk about serendipity. By dessert, she and Valerie had had them married and the parents of twins. "In the very best of families. He matches all your specifications. A stockbroker. Harvard graduate. He even takes Sunday brunch with his family." That, more than anything, spoke well of him, Rita thought.

"Oh?" Matrice leaned back, ignoring the nagging headache that was beginning to build up in her temples. "He probably looks like a toad, right?"

"Right. After the Princess kissed him. I've seen him, Mary Therese. He's beautiful. Dark hair, olive complexion, cheekbones models kill for. Size forty-two long if I'm not mistaken."

"Measuring him for the tuxedo already?"

"It never hurts to be prepared."

No, but it might hurt to be too premature. Matrice had her doubts that this man was as good-looking as her mother claimed, but in the long run, looks weren't really that important to her. After all, hadn't she gone out with men who could have been used as models for Adonis only to discover that they were egomaniacs, in love with their own images? Or overbearing, arrogant idiots used to getting their own way just because of their looks? There were any one of a wealth of character flaws that could be attributed to men who were incredibly handsome. She'd settle for character any day. Just not *a* character.

"Take it from me, darling, Scott diMarco is a perfect match for you."

Her mother was always given to oversimplification. "Mother, nothing is perfect."

"Except me."

Matrice smiled fondly. "Sorry. Except you." She went back to scrolling her screen. "So, when do I get to meet Mr. Wonderful. At the altar?"

"If you prefer."

It was meant to be a sarcastic remark. Matrice hurried to rectify it. She wasn't that busy. "No, I think I'd really like an introduction to the man sometime before the words, 'I do.'"

"Good, because he's going to be calling you." There was a momentary pause as Rita checked her watch at the other end. Valerie should have told him about Mary Therese by now. "Probably sometime around now, if he's not being whisked off to a meeting."

Just as her mother finished, Matrice's phone began to ring and the light next to the line her mother was on began to flash. It was almost eerie. "Speak of the devil."

"Mary Therese, is that any way to talk about your future husband?"

"I sincerely hope not." Matrice drew a fortifying breath. "Okay, Mother, this is probably the most sensible way to go." At any rate, it made sense on paper. And it had worked for generations of her ancestors. Maybe it would work for her at that.

"And you've always been such a sensible girl, darling. 'Bye."

Matrice had the distinct feeling that her mother's parting words were not altogether complimentary, that she was somehow disappointed in the predictability of her only offspring's life.

Maybe she was just imagining it. She shrugged, then jabbed the button beneath the flashing light.

"Matrice Crusoe."

Her voice took him back a second. Though it was low and made him think of whiskey served cold, there was something almost too businesslike about the tone. He smiled and shook his head. He never thought he'd say that, Scott mused. "Matrice, this is Scott diMarco."

It was a deep, resonant voice and she found herself liking it instantly. So far, so good. "Yes, I've been expecting your call."

All right, now what? Scott felt himself fidgeting inside. "I've never found myself in this sort of a situation before."

Matrice began forming a face out of paper clips, trying to take her mind off the purpose of the call. "No, neither have I."

There was silence. So far, she was as helpful as a flounder. "I thought perhaps the two of us might get together for lunch."

"My thoughts exactly." He sounded aloof, strained, but then, what did she expect? This wasn't exactly a routine situation, and besides, she wasn't looking for a talk-show host. With two paper clips for eyes, she nudged four more to form a frown.

Maybe she was better in person, he thought, pulling his calendar over toward him. He checked it against his schedule. It was crammed, as usual, but he did have an opening.

"I can pencil you in for one o'clock tomorrow for lunch at Stephen's." As he held his pencil poised, Scott frowned. Pencil you in? He had never used that expression before. Obviously, he'd been hanging around with the other brokers too much. He was beginning to sound like a yuppie. The idea of being a stereotype anything didn't sit well with him. Maybe he'd been working too hard at being a success and was losing sight of other things.

There was silence on the other end again. She certainly wasn't very talkative. He supposed there were advantages to that. He didn't want to have his ear chewed off. "One not good for you? Or is it the restaurant?"

Pencil her in. Oh, God, he sounded like a yuppie. That's all she needed. Another man involved in an intimate relationship with his BMW, his car phone and his Rolex.

Matrice bit her lower lips. She was being too judgmental. One phrase does not a shallow yuppie make, right?

"One's fine for me. You just go ahead and pencil me in, Scott." Try as she might, she couldn't keep the slight note of annoyance out of her voice. "I'll be there."

She sounded uptight, but maybe it had been a bad day for her, too. It certainly had been for him. Vowing to give this his best shot, Scott wrote her name in next to the only empty line on his calendar. "Fine, I'll see you then."

"Fine," she echoed, then hung up.

Not fine, she thought.

Matrice had a bad feeling about this. But then, maybe she was being too picky again. She had that habit. Maybe, but she doubted it.

Chapter Two

He had penciled her in for one o'clock.

The phrase, replaying itself in her head, grated on Matrice's nerves. It wasn't as if she hadn't heard it carelessly tossed about before. She had. Dozens of times. Everyone was *always* penciling in someone or something on their daily planners.

So why did it bother her so much this time?

Maybe, she mused, chewing on her lower lip, it was because it just didn't sound like an appropriate remark coming from a man about to meet the woman who would possibly be his future wife.

Maybe she was being too touchy. She was no longer in the market for romance, right? That *was* what this arrangement was all about. She was looking for a sensible, compatible match that would last long after the passion had evaporated. Her friend, Edie, had married in the heat of passion and, according to her, the passion had vanished as quickly as it had appeared, practically right after the honeymoon.

Matrice wasn't about to make a stupid mistake like that, rushing into a union that had failure written all over it, just because her hormones obstructed her good judgment. She had entrusted her future to the one person who placed her welfare and happiness before her own—her mother. And she had faith in her mother.

She was still telling herself that the next day at twelve-thirty. By now the statement was ringing a little hollow.

Matrice took her purse from the bottom desk drawer and shut off her computer. This was going to be all right. It was. Her generous mouth twisted slightly in an ironic smile. After all, she was penciled in, wasn't she?

A dark-haired woman in a dark gray suit knocked once on Matrice's door and leaned in, her palm balanced on the doorknob. "Gates wants to see you in the conference room at one-thirty."

Matrice shook her head as she rose from behind her desk. She was secure enough not to jump every time the senior partner snapped his fingers. It hadn't always been that way, but that was before she'd secured the Marlow account from very formidable competition.

"No can do, Gayle." Matrice tucked her purse under her arm. "I'm off to meet my husband-to-be." She had no idea why she was admitting this, especially to Gayle. Nerves, probably.

For once, the woman's lofty expression dissolved. "Husband? You're engaged?"

Only if her mother was on target. Still, it felt good to have Gayle guessing. "Sort of."

Gayle's pencil-thin body stood erect, centered in the doorway, blocking Matrice's only way out. "When did all this happen?"

Matrice glanced at her Rolex. If it hadn't been a gift from her mother, she wouldn't have been caught dead wearing it. But Matrice had a rule about gifts. They were not to be returned no matter what, even if they made her uncomfortable, which this one did. She knew the watch labeled her as being something she wasn't. It was bad enough that her life-style pointed toward her being a young, upwardly mobile professional. She didn't want to flaunt outward symbols.

"In fifteen minutes, if I can get a cab and traffic is actually moving out there." Stephen's was some ten city blocks uptown and she wasn't about to attempt to walk there in this heat.

Very thin eyebrows pulled together into a V as Gayle attempted to decipher hidden meanings. She stepped into Matrice's office. "Then you're *not* engaged?"

Matrice rather relished the look of total confusion on the woman's angular face. Gayle had an annoying penchant for acting smug and superior whenever she was privy to any information that hadn't reached Matrice, as well.

"Sort of," Matrice repeated, tossing the words over her shoulder as she hurried out. Figure *that* out, she added silently.

The air-conditioning system within the Mead Building was flawless and did an excellent job of making the muggy weather hanging over the city streets a distant memory. Preoccupied, Matrice was definitely not prepared for the assault of moist, hot air that hit her, casting her into the middle of a tropical rain forest atmosphere, as soon as she exited the revolving glass door into the street. The effect was instantaneous. She could feel her crisp, white linen suit immediately transform into a lead weight as the oppressive humidity seeped into every fiber of body and clothing.

Matrice fervently hoped that she could find an air-conditioned taxi and that she'd find it soon, before she completely melted down to nothing. She wasn't at her best when she was frazzled. Heat tended to curl her hair and shorten her temper. That was no frame of mind to be in when she made her first impression of Scott diAngelo—no, diMarco, she corrected herself.

If this works out, you have a lifetime to make a better impression.

Matrice tried to hold on to the thought that it was all going to work out for the best and to ignore the gnawing feeling at the pit of her stomach that she was stepping into another fiasco.

It was high time she got on with the rest of her life and filled out that corner that stood empty. She both needed and wanted to be married. To the right man. She had never plotted it out, never thought out that transitional jump from single career woman to married career woman with children, but she knew it was there for her. She had never really doubted it, except in the small, quiet moments in the middle of the night when she'd lie awake, staring at her ceiling, wondering what this whirlwind pace she was caught up in was all about.

The middle of the night seemed to be the time when all her insecurities would gather and rally around her, undermining her confidence about the future. At other times, in the light of day, she was certain it would happen. Eventually.

But eventually was beginning to breathe hot and heavy down her neck and she wanted a marriage to materialize. She was just at a loss as to how. Matrice was a wiz at details, but professional ones, not personal ones. That was her mother's forte.

She knew she could trust her mother.

The woman was late.

Scott found impatience beginning to nudge its way into his consciousness. He hated being kept waiting. It was one of his pet peeves. Valerie called it one of his failings, but he had a meeting to get to by two-thirty and even though his office was only four blocks away, he didn't like having to hurry through this first introduction to the rest of his life.

He fingered the chunky glass the waiter had brought him. A Scotch and soda. Scott frowned at it. Normally he didn't drink at lunch, but he had to admit that he felt uneasy, nervous. The drink gave him something to do with his hands when she got here. *If* she got here. Maybe she had thought better of the situation and had decided not to come.

Maybe he should do the same.

Just jitters, he told himself. It would pass. After all, this wasn't your everyday situation and he had no frame of reference to go by.

He glanced at his watch for the fourth time in five minutes. Well, one thing was for sure: he valued punctuality and obviously she didn't. Maybe they weren't as compatible as Val thought they were.

His attention was suddenly drawn to the entrance of the dining room as he heard a loud commotion. A patron had collided with a waiter and the tray the uniformed man had been carrying went flying to the floor with an enormous clatter. The patron, a woman in a white linen suit, narrowly escaped being christened with a hot serving of shrimp scampi. All except for her shoes, Scott noticed.

He watched, fascinated, as the young waiter dropped down to his knees and with a napkin began furiously wiping away the telltale streaks from her shoes.

Scott couldn't help wondering if the maneuver had somehow been engineered by the man just so he could get a different perspective of the woman's long, slender legs. They certainly were something to look at, even from where he sat.

No, on second thought, the way the woman was shaking that riot of dark brown hair at the waiter, the fault looked as if it belonged exclusively to her. So pretty and yet so clumsy, he mused.

Scott went back to toying with his drink. It was getting watered down as the ice cubes continued to melt beneath the amber liquid. He didn't have much patience with clumsy people, Scott thought, tilting the glass and watching it coat the thick sides.

He blew out a breath softly as he took a sip. Lately, it seemed as if he didn't have much patience at all. The toll of his profession, he imagined, yet he couldn't for the life of him see himself doing anything else. The bitter liquid slid down his throat, smooth, yet raw at the same time.

"Mr. diMarco?"

Scott raised his eyes at the sound of the low voice, first taking in the white linen skirt, then the almost imperceptible swell of the hip and lastly the subtle whiff of a fragrance that sold for seventy-five dollars an ounce.

"Scott?"

It was almost a full beat before Scott rose to his feet. The woman he had just watched having shrimp cleaned from her shoes was standing next to his table. This was his perfect match?

"Yes?" Maybe he was jumping to conclusions. Maybe his beeper wasn't working and she was just someone sent from his office to find him. But he didn't have much hope of that being true, unless she had been hired in the last half hour. He knew everyone at the office, at least by face if not by name, and he would have remembered this face. The creamy white skin framed by hair that was unruly, yet oddly sensuous. The wide blue eyes. He would have remembered the mouth alone. It was the kind that played on a man's mind and made him want to sample.

If anything, her mother had understated his good looks. He was almost *too* good-looking. Matrice didn't know if that was a strike against him or not.

Her queasiness returning, she extended her hand to him. "I'm Matrice Crusoe."

There wasn't an iota of recognition in his eyes. Nothing. Had she made a mistake? No, the maitre d' had pointed him out, after murmuring an apology about the inept class of help one managed to find these days.

His eyes were green, Matrice thought as the color swept through her. The kind of liquid green that was all but mesmerizing, if they had a spark of friendliness to them. These didn't—at least she couldn't detect it. Right now they seemed to be staring at her intently, as if he was waiting for her to say something further. Like what? "Will you marry me?"

She was just nervous. Taking a slow breath, she made herself calm down. This wasn't a fatal trap. She could walk out at any time. This meeting was just to approve the goods, so to speak.

She let go of his hand and gratefully slid into the chair that the waiter held out for her. The same waiter who had just cleaned her shoes. Was that an omen?

"I'm sorry I'm late." Was that what Scott was waiting for? An apology? It wasn't her fault. She spread her napkin out and noticed a tiny dot of red on her skirt. Maybe the cleaners could work a miracle. "Traffic wasn't moving."

"I walked."

Matrice raised her eyes to his face. Good for you, she thought, feeling a little testy. She shifted slightly as she accepted a menu from the waiter and realized that she hadn't escaped unscathed by the incident at the door. There was something squishy in her right shoe. Probably a shrimp.

Matrice closed her eyes for a moment. This was *not* shaping up as one of her better luncheons.

When she opened her eyes again, she saw that Scott was still looking at her. His expression was totally unreadable. "You walked here in this heat?"

Scott shrugged carelessly. "Heat doesn't bother me."

Great, he doesn't sweat, she thought irritably. Well, she did. She hated this hot weather and hated being late for an appointment. The incident at the door hadn't helped her disposition any, either. She felt her blood pressure rise by several notches.

"How fortunate for you." She kept her voice crisp. "My office is ten blocks away. If I'd walked, I probably wouldn't have made it." I would have melted by the third block, she added silently.

"Don't get much exercise?" he guessed. She looked to be in good condition, but clothes could camouflage a lot of defects. Adhering to an exercise regime was almost an obsession with Scott. Beside his family, it was the only thing that was important to him in his private life. He thought of Valerie. How could she have thought he'd be compatible with someone who didn't like exercise?

She didn't care for the tone of his voice when he'd asked that. It was condescending. Another yuppie who felt a person's worth was measured by the kind of annual membership dues they paid to a big-name health club.

"Yes." This time, she didn't bother to keep the iciness out of her voice. "As a matter of fact, I do. I just don't see the point in trotting around in unbearable weather, perspiring. Unlike you, I'm afraid I do that sort of thing."

She saw the waiter, who had approached at the tail end of the conversation, vainly trying to suppress a grin. It had been a snide remark and she knew it. But she wasn't sorry. He deserved it.

What was *her* problem? He'd been the one kept waiting. All he had done was draw a natural conclusion from her statement. Scott picked up his menu, wondering if another drink wasn't in order. "Let's order, shall we?"

She raised her menu before her like a shield. "Yes, let's."

It took him only a moment to decide. "I'll have the veal scaloppine."

"Make that two." Matrice surrendered her menu to the waiter.

"Will you care for something to drink?" the waiter asked her.

A gallon of white wine to anesthetize myself from Mr. Wonderful. "I'll have a Scotch and soda."

Scott raised a brow. That wasn't a usual choice for a woman. She favored the same meal, the same drink as he did. Scott decided to regroup. He was here. He might as well make the best of it. Maybe she was one of those people who made a terrible first impression and got better as time went on. "Well, at least we agree on something."

She didn't care for the way he said that. It sounded too sarcastic. "According to my mother, we agree on a lot of things."

"Your mother?" With all the things going on today, he'd forgotten that Valerie had said she knew this woman's mother. He had some faceless woman to blame for what he was enduring right now. As well as himself.

There was that note of condescension in his voice again. She could feel her hackles rising. "Yes, my mother. She 'found you,' so to speak."

He didn't care for being made to sound as if he was some sort of a door prize to be raffled off to an overachieving, biological clock conscious woman. One hand tightening on his drink, he leaned forward. "Tell me, why would a woman like you need her mother to find her a husband?"

He was laughing at her. The waiter set her drink in front of her and Matrice briefly entertained the idea of seeing Scott picking ice cubes out of his perfectly combed hair.

"Because—" Matrice consciously refrained from gritting her teeth together "—a woman like *me* doesn't have the time to mingle and endure searching through a lot of fool's gold to get the real thing."

He had the distinct impression she was lumping him in with the former. He hadn't wanted romance. At least, he hadn't thought he did until just this moment. This whole setup was too antiseptic for him. And she was too caustic. He had a vision of her, dressed like a 'forty-niner, panning for gold at Sutter's Mill—except rather than sand and grit, there were tiny men in her pan and she was picking through them, tossing them aside one by one. "And that's important to you."

"Isn't it to you?" She thought that was why they were here. "According to my—"

"—mother," he filled in. This time there was a definite baiting note in his voice.

Matrice gripped the glass tighter in her hand. "Yes, according to her, you're very success and goal oriented."

She said it as if it was a character flaw. He raised his glass and toasted her with the remains of his drink. "As are you."

Why did she get the feeling that they were engaged in some sort of sophisticated name-calling? She knew she should have listened to the sinking feeling in her stomach and not come. This whole thing had been doomed from the start.

"There's nothing wrong with wanting to succeed," she said tersely.

"No, there isn't." But a wife, he was beginning to realize, was not obtained the same way he had gone about everything else in his life. She wasn't a goal to be achieved.

You couldn't just place an order over the counter and be satisfied with your acquisition. There were other things involved. Important things. Logic alone wasn't enough in making a choice, a commitment of this nature.

Look what he had gotten by going that route.

Scott turned his attention to the meal the waiter brought him, suddenly needing a breather from the woman who sat opposite him.

Matrice tried to remember when she had ever felt so awkward before. The answer was never.

"So, why are you looking into an arranged marriage?" she finally asked, when the silence grew to be too unbearable for her to handle.

He could almost detect the smirk behind her question. Obviously she thought there was something wrong with a man who would look to other channels for finding a mate.

Even though he had just admitted as much to himself, he grew defensive. If there was something wrong with a man like that, what did that make her for wanting one who went that route?

"Same reason. Too busy," he told her.

Blue eyes regarded green. "It does seem as if we have things in common."

"Yes, it does." On paper. There wasn't a thing about her that he felt was reflected in himself. He wasn't as cold and calculating as she was. Or as snide. And he'd like to believe that he would die before being that smug.

So far, she had had better conversations with her dog. At least Travis barked in the right places. "So, you work for Sperry, Dun and Brinkwater."

"Yes. And you work for Atkinson, Mayer and Brown."

"Yes."

God, this was beginning to be painful, Scott thought. They were exchanging verbal business cards. He was hard-pressed to remember when he had been in a more boring conversation.

It came to him in a flash of lightning. She was beautiful, she was educated and undoubtedly she knew all the right people. But it just wasn't enough. It wasn't enough to make it work.

A throbbing, staccato noise broke the painful silence between them.

Matrice nodded toward the sound. "Don't look now, but I think your jacket is trying to get your attention."

He withdrew a black, palm-size object from his inside pocket. "It's my beeper."

Did he think she was an idiot? She'd only been making a joke. "I know what it is."

Good for you, he thought. "I'll only be a minute." He rose to find a phone.

"Don't hurry on my account. Please," she added the last word under her breath.

Letting out a sigh at the momentary reprieve, Matrice took a few bites of her lunch. For the first time since the waiter had served it, the food didn't feel as if it was sticking to the roof of her mouth. She was definitely going to give her mother a piece of her mind about taking advantage of her daughter's momentary lapse of common sense.

He was back all too soon.

"Emergency all cleared up?" she asked brightly.

He wondered if she'd majored in sarcasm at school. This had to have been what Shakespeare had in mind when he'd written about Kate the Shrew, except God help the man who tried to tame this one.

"Just some last-minute details about the Marlow account," he told her, sitting down.

"Rodell Marlow?"

"Yes." He was surprised she knew the name of his former client. And then it came to him. "That's right, your company lured him away from mine.'' He knew it was a volatile choice of words as soon as he'd said it, but there was no regret.

"We didn't 'lure' him away, we gave him a better deal. He's one of my chief priorities now,'' she added, purposely sounding smug.

Scott lost the last shred of his appetite. "He's *your* client?''

That almost tore it. "You say that as if you don't think I can handle him.''

Satisfied that his meaning was apparent, he gracefully left the battlefield. "I didn't say that.''

"You were, however, thinking it.''

He smiled at her innocently. "Is that how you got Marlow?''

What was he babbling about? "What?''

"Reading minds.''

She took a minute to regroup. It was foolish, she thought, of the restaurant to leave sharp objects around and then allow infuriating apes to share meals with the rest of the clientele.

Scott almost shuddered. To think what he had almost done because he was too busy to take charge of his private life. What if he'd gone into this blindly, the way instinct had first suggested, and left everything up to Valerie to handle? What if this was a hundred years ago in the old country and he had met this shrew at the altar just before they'd exchanged their vows?

Thank God for progress.

God, what a mistake she had almost made. Married, to him? She couldn't think of anything more odious than having that smug, walking ticker tape touch her, claiming "husbandly rights.''

The waiter quietly asked them if there would be anything else. The mutual, resounding no that met his question had him hurrying to return with the check.

Matrice raised an eyebrow as she saw Scott's hand go out.

Oh, no. This was a lesson she'd be glad to pay for and be done with it. He wasn't going to go back to the office and complain that she had soaked him for lunch. "I'll get it," she declared.

Was she trying to top him at this, too? Manners had taught him to pay for a lady, and she wasn't about to interfere with that, even though he felt as if he was stretching the term to apply it to her. "No, that's all right. I'll pay."

"I said, let me—"

Her eyes fixed on his, Matrice reached for the silver tray that contained the bill and accidentally knocked over Scott's water glass.

"What the—?" He yelped in surprise as ice water hit his lap in the most uncomfortable place it could find. She probably had it trained, he thought, glaring at her as he yanked over the napkin he had just tossed aside on the table.

Matrice bit her lower lip, this time to keep from laughing. Maybe she had a guardian angel hovering around after all.

"On second thought, Scott, I think I'll let you pay." She rose. "I have to get to a meeting with Mr. Marlow." She didn't, but she enjoyed the annoyed look that her statement generated. "We'll stay in touch," she promised, slipping her purse under her arm.

The hell we will. "Sure thing." Scott sopped up the water with his napkin. How was he supposed to return to the office looking like this?

When hell freezes over. Matrice turned on her heel and walked out, the shrimp squishing in her shoe. She didn't even notice. Life was built up of small triumphs in the face of disasters.

Chapter Three

Matrice had every intention of chastising her mother in person for the horrid luncheon she had been made to endure. How her mother could think she and Scott were made for each other—no, her mother had said they were almost identical in nature—seriously bothered Matrice. Did her mother have such a low opinion of her?

But then the yen went up and suddenly the pins were being knocked out from beneath several highly rated, popular stocks. She stayed late at the office, trying to make some sense out of the ensuing chaos, and went home to her dog and her economy-size bottle of extra-strength aspirin.

She took one tablet, fed Travis and then took two more, wondering if her stomach lining was being eaten away at a prodigious rate. Lately, she had been consuming aspirin as if they were candy.

If she wasn't careful, Matrice warned herself, she was going to have yet another unwanted symbol of the upper-wardly mobile professional. An ulcer.

Matrice returned the aspirin bottle to her medicine cabinet, walked into the living room and called her mother. If she waited for her headache to go away, it would be the middle of next year before she could speak to her mother and tell her the gory details of the luncheon date from hell.

Rita Crusoe listened patiently for five minutes as Matrice elaborately told her just what she thought of Scott diMarco and his parentage. When Matrice paused for breath, Rita wearily asked, "Then I'm to take it that this first meeting didn't go well?"

Matrice sank down on her love seat and stretched her legs out on the cushions. "You always were given to understatements, Mother. And it wasn't the first meeting. It was the *only* meeting. I never want to see that man again."

"But why?" Rita didn't understand how Matrice could be so turned off by Scott. He seemed so right for her. "You told me what you were looking for in a husband. Scott has all the right qualifications."

Matrice closed her eyes and dropped her head back, resting it against the cushion. It didn't help. It just shifted the pain. "Pinocchio had all the right parts to be a real boy, but he was still made of wood."

Rita had never heard her daughter sound so incensed about a date before. "Just what *did* happen at lunch?" Nothing Mary Therese had said so far seemed worthy of generating such a vehement response.

Unless of course...

Rita began toying with a thought.

Travis jumped onto Matrice's lap, making her wince. Her head began to pound harder. "Do the words *major disaster* conjure up any pictures?"

Yes, but the idea Rita had just come up with was creating a much more vivid one. "Mary Therese, I really think—"

Matrice was intimately familiar with that tone. It was best to put an abrupt end to this conversation before her mother had time to develop whatever germ of an idea had just popped into her head. There was no telling where her mother would go with this, given her head. "—that you have had better ideas."

No, Rita sincerely doubted it. "Perhaps if you give him another chance..." Rita began slowly.

Matrice sat up, her head defining the motion in short, stabbing throbs. Momentarily defeated, she sank back into the sanctuary of the love seat.

"Nope. No way. Uh-uh." Travis licked her hand, as if empathizing with whatever it was that was troubling his mistress.

The more Mary Therese talked, the more certain Rita became that her initial suspicion was correct. "You certainly are adamant about it."

"I will be obsessive about it if you want. The man doesn't sweat."

Maybe her daughter was working too hard. "That's not exactly an offense punishable by jail, darling."

Scott wasn't worth getting annoyed over, but Matrice couldn't help herself. Each word cost her as it echoed in her head. "He's an android, Mother. A sarcastic, pompous, arrogant, egotistical Ivy League jerk."

It was hard not to laugh. "Does have your blood up, doesn't he?"

Matrice could understand why her father had often called her mother the most stubborn woman on the face of the earth. She just refused to let go.

"I know what you're thinking and you're wrong. I react the same way to red ants." Matrice tried again, attacking the problem on a different level. "Mother, if I married him—" she stifled a shiver "—I'd have to go to bed with him."

Rita didn't bother hiding the smile in her voice. "That is the general idea, no?"

"No!" Matrice's hand flew to her head, as if that could stop the onslaught of pain generated by the single word she had shouted. "No," she whispered, reinforcing the word softly. "Not if he was the last man on earth. Not if I was shipwrecked on a desert island with just him for the rest of my life. I'd rather throw myself into a volcano."

The word *island* caught Rita's attention. What if—?

"They only do that with virgins, darling." Rita's smile grew as her plan took on breadth and substance. Gerald had an island. He had grandiose plans to someday develop it into a miniparadise that was close to him.

Matrice sighed. And to think she had been expecting sympathy. "Don't get cute, Mother."

"Cute? I have never been cute, darling. Stunning, perhaps, but not cute." Rita began to weave her web, taking care not to sound too eager. She didn't want Mary Therese to suspect anything, but it was hard keeping her enthusiasm in check. "Speaking of islands, I'd like you to help me make up my mind about something."

Matrice was too tired to think, too tired to construct coherent thought about anything except how soon she could drop, facedown, into bed. If she was very lucky, maybe God would cancel tomorrow. "What?"

"Purchasing one."

Now she knew her mind was wandering. "What?"

"There's this small island up for sale, just off Nantucket." She knew she could talk her cousin into letting her use it for the weekend. It would be perfect. As long as Valerie managed her part. "Come with me?"

Matrice was usually very game to take part in one of her mother's ventures. But she had just come away from one scathed, and it would take a bit of time for her to work up enthusiasm about another. Especially when she wasn't even certain she would live till morning.

"I don't know anything about islands, Mother, small or otherwise. Besides, the only island you've ever shown any interest in is Manhattan."

"I believe in growing. I'm looking into this as investment property. A getaway. We'll learn together," Rita said cheerfully. "It'll do you good to get away after this horrible experience you've just had."

Well, at least her mother was agreeing with her on that. It was a small victory. "You've got a point there," Matrice murmured.

"Of course I do. Settled?" And if it wasn't, she'd argue until it was. Rita Crusoe did not take no for an answer easily. Or ever.

Matrice sighed again and tried to drag her hand through her hair. The roots of her hair ached. "If I'm free."

"Be free, darling. Be free."

Pleased, Rita broke the connection, then tapped out the familiar numbers to Valerie's penthouse apartment. She had to sound her out on the idea. As she listened to the phone ring, she smiled. Mary Therese's reaction to Scott had been strong. Strong enough to make her suspect that the old adage about where there's smoke, there's fire was more than just something Bartlett had used to pad out his book of quotations.

There had been no time to call Valerie while he was at the office. Scott pressed her number on his automatic dialer as soon as he walked through the door of his apartment. "Val, Scott. I thought you might want to know how things went."

"I've been waiting by my phone all afternoon."

"Please, no guilt trips, Val." He loosened his tie and opened the top button of his shirt. "To put it simply, it was an unqualified disaster." Though she didn't say a word, he could hear her disappointment. "Sorry, Val, you tried." Juggling the phone from one hand to the other, he shed his jacket and slung it over the back of the sofa. "It was a stupid idea on my part to even think things could be done that way."

Matrice had seemed so perfect for him. What had gone wrong? "But what did she do?"

He gave a short laugh as he recalled the meeting. "After she walked into the waiter or before?"

Bracing herself, Valerie said, "Before."

He glanced down at his answering machine. The red light indicated three messages. He'd call them back tomorrow. He was in no mood to be friendly tonight. "She was late for lunch."

Valerie shook her head. Scott was too tense. There had been a time when a few minutes hadn't mattered to him. "Deadly sin number eight. And after?"

Scott frowned, remembering the look on Matrice's face when she'd told him about Marlow. "She was defensive, opinionated and excessively competitive."

What did that mean? "She arm wrestled you?"

"Only for the check."

"Excuse me?"

"Poor joke." Annoyed, he yanked his tie completely off, then, thinking better of it, draped it next to his jacket on the sofa. There was no use taking the afternoon out on his clothes. "But she did upset the water glass when she tried to snatch the check away from me."

Valerie tried not to sound as if she was grinning. "I see."

"No," he said, settling himself on the sofa and trying to drain the tension from his body. It usually worked. Tonight, though, the tension refused to leave. Small wonder. "No, I don't think you do. But you should have." He shook his head. "She was like a mongoose, attacking."

"Were you the egg or the snake?"

"Neither. Just the innocent bystander in this case." His eyes strayed toward the bar. If ever there had been a day that warranted a drink to help him unwind, it was this one. He dragged himself off the sofa again. "No, I'm afraid that as far as marriage goes, it has to be done the new old-fashioned way instead of the old old-fashioned way. Trial and error. Something I don't have time for."

He made her despair. "You'll keep saying that until it's too late, Scott."

He cradled the phone against his shoulder as he reached with one hand for a glass beneath the bar. With the other, he took the bottle of wine he had chilled in the small refrigerator he kept there. "Then I'll always have you and Frank and the gang." He glanced at the framed photograph of his brother's family that he kept on the side table.

"That's not enough."

He poured, measuring out just the right amount, then returned the bottle to the refrigerator. "'Fraid it'll have to do."

Valerie couldn't shake the feeling that Scott was being too hasty. "Did she feel the same way about you?"

He took a sip, felt it go down and then laughed. "I'd bet on it."

"How could you tell?"

"There are ways." He took another sip to strengthen his opinion. "The smoke coming out of her ears and the way she ran off right after lunch, to name two."

There was silence on the other end and Scott thought that perhaps Val was mulling over defeat. Her next question came out of the blue. "What was she wearing?"

Now what brought that on? Valerie wasn't the type to really care what people wore. "Clothes."

"Very funny. What kind of clothes?"

"I don't know." More silence told him that Valerie was still waiting for an answer. To please her, he gave it some thought. "A white linen suit." He grinned. "And shrimp scampi shoes."

She was right. He was working much too hard these days. He needed a break. And a wife. The *right* wife. And though he protested vigorously, Valerie was certain she had found that woman for him. If only he'd stay sane. "What are you talking about?"

"The waiter she bumped into dropped an order of shrimp scampi and some of it splattered on her shoes. He practically groveled at her feet as he wiped it up." Now that he had met her, he thought he was a fair judge of Matrice's reaction to it. "She must have enjoyed that."

"Anything else?" Valerie prodded, proving a point to herself.

He shrugged, more to himself than in response to her question. "The skirt kind of brushed up against her knees. She had on a plum-colored silk blouse. And she wore her hair loose. Like a dark sky before the storm." He realized that he'd conjured Matrice up a little too vividly in his mind's eye. Quickly he dismissed the image. There was no use dwelling on the unpleasant. "*She* was the storm. Anything else?"

"No, I think you've told me enough."

Now what was that supposed to mean? He was about to ask her when the tiny beep within the phone interrupted. "I've got another call, Scottie."

He took it as a reprieve. He needed a hot shower. A long one. "That's all right. I've got some things to do before I turn in tonight."

Val depressed the receiver and took the next call. "Hello, Rita," she said without waiting to hear the other person's voice.

Stunned silence met her and then she heard Rita's surprised voice. "How did you know?"

Valerie laughed. "Just a hunch. I just finished talking to Scott. Wow."

"My sentiments exactly. Mary Therese gave me an earful, too." Rita got down to the heart of the matter. "So, what do you think?"

Valerie could tell by the older woman's tone that she was in agreement with her. "There's a lot going on here. He's much too adamant, too passionate on the subject of how wrong she is for him. I've never heard him like this before."

"That's what I felt with Mary Therese. There's a fire here."

"So, what do you propose we do?"

Rita smiled broadly to herself. "Fan it."

The sea breeze ruffled Matrice's hair, sending it every which way. She tried unsuccessfully to make it behave, then gave up. "I really don't think this is such a good idea, Mother." She turned to face the woman who had all but shanghaied her out here. "I really have a ton of work to do."

Rita waved the statement away, taking absolutely no note of it. "You always have work to do." She put her arm around Mary Therese's slim shoulders. The girl could eat more. "Getting away for the weekend will do you good, darling. Trust me."

Matrice could feel her stomach lurching with every rough wave that swayed the boat. "Getting seasick won't." She pressed a hand to her stomach. "Shouldn't we have a crew or something?" She looked around, as if that would make them materialize.

Rita sniffed as she returned to the wheel. "I'm an excellent navigator." John had taught her. Some things, you never forgot. Rita glanced at her daughter. Things like the touch of a husband's hand, reaching for you late at night, just to hold you. She wanted that for Mary Therese.

Matrice joined her on unsteady legs. "You're an 'excellent' con artist."

"Is that any way to talk to your mother?" Rita held her hand steady on the wheel. They'd be there soon.

"It is if your mother's a con artist." Matrice looked at her pointedly. "And you are." Shading her eyes, she squinted at the horizon. A small stretch of something rested on the blue waters like a drop of sand the wind had forgotten to clear away. "Is that it?"

Rita kept her eyes fixed on the island and she navigated the boat for shore. "Yes."

"Looks tiny."

"I thought I'd start small."

Matrice looked at her mother suspiciously. "Gilligan's Island was bigger."

"It had to support more people. I thought that I'd only give small, intimate parties on it."

"I thought it was for investment purposes."

"I haven't completely made up my mind yet." Rita hoped that Mary Therese would forgive her when the time came for such things.

"You're serious about this."

Rita never wavered. "I've always wanted to own my own island."

It still made no sense to Matrice. Her mother had never talked about this before. Never even so much as mentioned it. "Why?"

The elegant shoulder rose and fell casually. "Why do you want a seat on the stock exchange?"

Obviously, she wasn't going to get a straight answer from her. "One has nothing to do with the other."

Rita looked at her only daughter for a long moment. "Dreams are always alike."

"Not all of them." Matrice sighed, thinking of things she had somehow missed along the way in her hurry to get to the top. Lately, that had been nagging at her, that feeling that chanted, "Is this all there is?" Maybe it was just her biological clock, or maybe it was her life ticking away. Matrice didn't know, but somehow, everything she had wasn't enough.

And yet, each day was a scramble, a mad whirlwind just to keep up, to maintain. To persevere, to keep going with that world of men on Wall Street and find her own niche.

Maybe her mother was right. Maybe she *did* need a break, a weekend to get away.

Matrice suddenly became aware that the boat had headed in straight for the island. Her mother had cut the engine. "What are you doing?"

Rita climbed out of the boat and into the water before she answered. There was a very small dock about fifteen feet in length running along the edge of the island. It was the only sign of civilization that Matrice could detect.

"Docking."

Matrice jumped out after her, though she would have rather stayed in the boat. "Why?"

Rita paused long enough to pat Mary Therese's cheek. "To see the island."

Matrice threw up her hands. "We saw it. From the boat." And there wasn't much to look at as far as she was concerned. Just sand and a few trees.

Rita shook her head. "You can't make up your mind without looking around, without giving it a chance."

"I can." Matrice folded her arms in front of her stubbornly. She had some out to see the island and she had seen it. And from what she could see, there wasn't anything to get excited about.

"That might be your problem." The words were said very quietly.

Matrice let her arms drop to her sides. "You're not talking about the island, are you?"

The rounded face strove for innocence. "What else would I be referring to?"

They both knew exactly what Rita was referring to—what had been on her mother's mind since she'd first called to set up the meeting between her and Scott. "That cold fish in the Armani suit. Scott what's-his-name."

"DiMarco," Rita supplied automatically. She tramped up the beach just far enough from the dock to lull Mary Therese's senses. "And just how do you know he's a cold fish?"

Matrice kept pace with her, although she had no idea where they were going. There didn't seem to be anything here. "I know, that's all."

Rita pressed her lips together and shook her head. She pulled her captain's hat lower over her eyes. "Seems to me, you don't give a lot of things a chance, Mary Therese."

Matrice shrugged. There was still something within her that wanted parental approval. She supposed there always would be. But she could live without it if necessary. "Some things you just know."

Lightly Rita ran her hand over Matrice's hair. "Yes, you do." She glanced down at her watch.

"Why do you keep looking at your watch?"

Rita dropped her hand to her side. "Am I?"

"You know you are. You've looked at it three times since we got off the boat."

Rita pretended to be preoccupied as she looked out at the sea. "Just thinking about when the tide is supposed to go out." And if Valerie had arrived on the other side of the island yet.

"Why, does the island sink then?" She wouldn't doubt it. Matrice looked around. "This really isn't very big at all."

"Two square miles," Rita informed her. She pointed toward the left. "There's a small shack just around that pile of sand."

Matrice looked. "Dune, Mother. If you're going to own it, call it by its name."

Rita was not one to be cowed. "I can call it Irving if I want." She rolled it around in her head. "Irving. Catchy name."

Her mother was beginning to sound as if she needed this weekend getaway more than she did, Matrice thought. "For an island?"

"Why not?" She pointed toward the dune. "Why don't you go check out the shack?"

"And what are you going to do?" Matrice asked suspiciously.

"Make sure I secured the boat. We wouldn't want to get marooned here."

"God forbid."

Rita waved her away. "Now go. The walk'll do you good. Might take the edge off that tart tongue of yours."

Matrice wiped her brow. It felt as if it was ninety in the shade and there was precious little of that. "A tall glass of bottled water'll do that."

Rita nodded. "I'll be sure to take out the ice chest, darling, while I'm at it. Now go, explore. Live up to the Crusoe name."

Matrice stopped in her tracks. "That was fiction, Mother."

"No, it was actually based on fact. Defoe read an article in the newspaper. Stole your kinsman's story. No such thing as copyright in those days, really."

The woman was a storehouse for some rather useless information. But that was what made her so unique. And endearing. Even in ninety-degree weather. "There's one thing I want to know."

Rita stiffened. Did she suspect? "What?"

"Who gets to be Friday?"

Slowly Rita let out the breath she'd been holding. "See if you can find us a native for the part."

Matrice looked surprised. "There're people on this island?"

The smile on her mother's face was mysterious. "Not yet."

"What does that mean?"

"My parties, remember?" Rita asked, the soul of innocence again.

"How can I forget?" Matrice sighed heavily and trudged off to find the house her mother seemed so eager for her to see.

It was a shack. A thatched ruin. Something that looked as if it had been constructed by backward natives in order to get out of the sun. Matrice circled it, refusing to go in. She heard a droning noise and wondered if mosquitoes were part of the island decor. The entire shack was the size of her bedroom. What was going on? If her mother thought she was going to enjoy spending any time here, the two of them had gotten more out of touch than she thought.

Swinging around, Matrice trudged back around the dune. It had taken them an hour and a half to get out here on the boat. If they set off immediately, they could make it back before two.

The boat was gone.

Matrice sucked in her breath as she stared at the empty dock. She began to run toward it. Maybe something had happened to the boat. But how could it have capsized? Wouldn't she have heard something? A scream? A—

The droning noise she had heard while she was inspecting the hut. That had sounded like—

A boat, starting up. She couldn't have!

Could she?

Squinting, Matrice shaded her eyes again and scanned the waters. She saw the boat then, bobbing up and down on the ocean. Her mother had spied her and was waving. Easily, not like a woman in distress.

She had *left* her here. Why?

As Matrice ran in the direction of the water, she tripped over the ice chest. She landed facedown in the sand. Sputtering, brushing the sand furiously off her face, she sat back and stared at the pile in front of her. An ice chest, a box of what looked like a few provisions and a makeup case with a note taped to it. Matrice glared at the makeup case. Her mother had gone senile in the space of a day.

Angry, frustrated, she ripped the note off the case and read it. "Darling, this is for the best. Trust me."

What? What was for the best? And why was her mother deserting her on this godforsaken sandbar?

Matrice crumpled up the note and made to throw it away, then shoved it into her pocket instead. Why had her mother done this? Was she trying to make some kind of a point? To get her to relax? How could she relax, marooned here? And for how long?

Upset, Matrice scrambled to her feet. Needing to vent her frustration, she kicked the sand and watched it spray around her toes. There was absolutely no satisfaction in that. She was hot, tired, irritated and marooned. God, how awful could things get?

A glimmer of green behind the ice chest flashed and caught her eye. She bent over and picked up a bottle that had fallen over when she'd knocked over the ice chest. Matrice stared at it incredulously.

"Mouthwash. What in heaven's name am I supposed to do with mouthwash? Who the hell is around that I could possibly offend?"

A noise behind her made Matrice swing around, her heart pounding. She clutched at her throat as her eyes grew wide with recognition. And shock.

"Oh my God."

Scott diMarco was walking toward her.

Chapter Four

Matrice stared, wide-eyed as the man in the distance walked over the rise of sun-bleached grass toward her. As he approached, shock evolved into total disbelief, which in turn was displaced by anger. Actually, *anger* might have been too mild a word for it. Heads were going to roll for this. She wasn't exactly sure whose just yet, but they were going to roll.

Filling her lungs full of air, like a steam engine burning through cords of wood for energy, Matrice scrambled to her feet. She stomped, as well as she could, across the beach toward Scott. Her eyes narrowed against the glare of the sun as she kept them focused on the tall figure ahead of her, like an arrow heading for a target.

He looked entirely different from the man who had sat across from her during that disastrous lunch they'd shared at Stephen's. He was wearing faded, frayed beige cutoffs that clung to his hips as if held there by sheer force of will. The old blue T-shirt he wore strained vainly against sculpted pectorals and biceps that resembled rock formations. The only reprieve the material got was when it stretched down the length of his torso toward his stomach. There it was flat. Absolutely, enticingly flat.

Presented with this image, Matrice's indignation began to mellow. Then she focused in on his face. He was just as handsome as she remembered, even more so. Yet that pompous arrogance was still there. She could see it in the tilt of his head.

Damn his hide, he had to somehow be responsible for all of this. This was probably his way of getting even with her for that glass of water she'd accidentally spilled on his lap. What could he have possibly told her mother to have made her agree to doing something like this?

Scott frowned as he cut the distance between them in long strides, the sand spraying to either side beneath his feet. He had already ascertained that Matrice was a royal pain, but he'd had no idea that she was this devious, as well. That just went to show him how he could underestimate a woman, even in this day and age. After all, he reminded himself, she *had* stolen the Marlow account from his firm. From him.

In his hand he still clutched the note he had found on top of the small ice chest beneath the tree. Valerie had sent him looking for the chest, saying she had left it there earlier. She'd told him that she wanted to tie the boat to the dock first before joining him. He'd thought it strange when she refused his help, but had let the matter go. Like a fool he had let her play sailor and went off in search of the ice chest. The search hadn't taken him long. The island was small and there weren't that many trees to be found on it.

The note aroused his curiosity. A single word was written on it: "Surprise." Just what did she mean by that?

When he turned to the dock to ask her about it and neither she nor the single-engined boat were there, Scott had a sneaking suspicion that he had his answer.

Or thought he did.

He began walking along the shoreline. Maybe Val had just decided to dock the boat someplace farther down, and this was all just some sort of game she was playing. It certainly wasn't like her.

He'd been stunned by his first view of Matrice. She was sitting beside another ice chest and some other paraphernalia he couldn't make out.

It was then that Scott realized that he really didn't have a clue to the answer. He'd thought that Valerie had left him here for his "own good," as she was fond of saying. To get away from the maddening crowds for a weekend and back in touch with himself. Now he realized that Valerie had conspired with this she-devil to see how quickly he could be driven completely crazy. Why? It made absolutely no sense. The so-called date had been a disaster and he had come away with a feeling that Matrice wanted to have as little to do with him as he with her.

So what the hell was going on? Why had he been left here with her?

Sure, the woman looked like someone he'd like to be shipwrecked with. With long, slender legs barely topped off with white cotton shorts and a flimsy pink halter that could be quickly dispensed with by one tug properly applied at the right moment, she was easily the most compellingly attractive woman he had ever seen. But he had already had the dubious privilege of talking with her. He knew firsthand the miserable disposition that lived within that attractively packaged body.

The hound from hell would have made a more desirable island companion.

Matrice propped her fisted hands on her hips. "This your idea of a joke, diMarco?" she snapped as soon as he was within range.

Ah, the shrew speaks. He gave her a very tight smile. "I was just about to ask you the same question, *Crusoe.*" He echoed her tone as he said her last name.

Matrice raised one brow. The insufferable egotist was probably going to feign ignorance and accuse her of orchestrating this ridiculous charade just to be alone with him. "No, this is my idea of a nightmare."

Maybe she wasn't behind this after all. She sounded too angry about it and she didn't strike him as being a good actress. That left Valerie, and he didn't like the thoughts he was having. Had she actually done this to him on purpose? Marooned him with this woman? How *could* she have done that to him?

Scott inclined his head with a nod. "Maybe we do have some things in common after all."

So now he was saying that being alone with her was his idea of a nightmare. Matrice squared her shoulders and attempted to stand taller than her five feet, one inches allowed her to. Without heels, she felt almost dwarfed by Scott as he came to a stop next to her.

"Maybe," she bit off. "The point is, what do we do about being stranded out here?"

Scott glanced past her head and toward the ocean. It was calm and peaceful, unlike what he was experiencing at this moment. It was also endless, or looked that way from where he stood. *Damn it, Val, what were you thinking?* "Well, swimming for shore is obviously out."

Wonderful. They were stuck out here and he was invoking what little wit he seemed to possess. She eyed him suspiciously, not entirely ready to give up her theory that he was behind this for his own perverse reasons. "So is falling into each other's arms."

Ha, that would be the day. Sorry, Val, you're as wrong as you can be about this one. Scott looked down into Matrice's eyes. The color of the ocean he had just been looking at, they made him think of the sea right before a storm. "Not even during a tidal wave."

The beast. She might not want to fall into his arms, but what was so wrong with hers? "Okay, so we understand each other?"

"As well as can be hoped for."

Matrice let out the last of the breath she had sucked in. She rocked on her heels, for the moment temporarily smothering the anger that vibrated within. No, he probably hadn't had a hand in this. There was feminine logic at work here.

She crossed her arms, as if attempting to physically contain her anger. "Your sister-in-law?" she guessed, thinking of the way her mother had tricked her into coming.

"And your mother." It wasn't a question on his part. It was all ridiculously clear now. How could he have not seen it coming? He thought of the innocent look on Valerie's face as she'd suggested this elaborate outing. "She said she wanted to check this out as a possible resort."

Matrice didn't even realize that Scott was talking about Valerie since her mother had used the same ploy. Her mother's face suddenly materialized in her mind at his statement. A sense of betrayal telegraphed itself through Matrice. How *could* she?

"And I fell for it." Matrice shook her head as she dragged a hand through her hair. She looked around. Marooned. Here. With him. Oh, God. "If I hadn't been so stressed out, I would have realized that none of this made any sense." Her mother didn't belong on an island any more than she belonged on an ice cake, floating in the Arctic Ocean.

He should have listened to his inner instincts and said no when he'd wanted to. But this had been Val and there was little he refused her.

"Well, I realize that it didn't make sense," he said, thinking aloud. It hadn't made sense, but he'd thought that perhaps Valerie needed to get away for some reason.

There he went, trying to be one up on her. "Oh? Well if you saw through this ruse, what are you doing here? Or do you like being marooned?"

Gamecocks had better dispositions than this woman. "I was indulging Val. People do that with people they care about." He felt his temper rising. The woman probably didn't know the first thing about caring selflessly for a person. "Of course, you probably wouldn't know about things like that."

Another barb. She was getting very tired of this, and him. Matrice unconsciously raised herself on her toes. She gained no leverage. "And just what are you trying to say?"

Overhead, a sea gull called to a mate. Scott strained to hear the sound of a motor growing louder as it returned to the island. He heard none. Damn. Another layer of his temper slipped by the wayside.

Knowing that if he continued to stand here, looking at that pugnacious lift to her chin, he'd be tempted to clip it, Scott turned and took several steps, then stopped. Where was he going to go? "If you're the Harvard grad Valerie claims you are, you can figure that out for yourself."

Oh, no, he wasn't about to walk away from her, leaving that insinuation hanging in the air. "Valerie doesn't have to 'claim' anything, I *am* a Harvard graduate." She placed her hand on his shoulder and pulled, making him swing around to face her. "I am also a lady, otherwise, you'd be doubled over on the ground right now with searing pain traveling through what you probably think are popular parts of your anatomy."

He eyed her coldly, but he did have the presence of mind to take a step back.

There was nothing to be gained by sniping at each other. He tried to forget that this woman had a way of annoying him beyond distraction, and attempted a different approach. Maybe if he credited her with some intelligence, she'd stop going for the jugular. "So, what do you suggest we do?"

Matrice was taken aback. She hadn't expected him to actually ask her a civilized question. Her answer was automatic. "Plot their collective murders, for openers." She shook her head as she looked out on the wide ocean. A feeling for desolation, not to mention frustration, swept through her. She had *things* to do, damn it, she couldn't just hang around here. "What in God's name could they have been thinking of?"

"I don't know," he admitted. "I never thought of Valerie as simpleminded before." He tried to be kind. This *was* the woman who had raised him when she'd been under no obligation to do so. "I guess everyone's entitled to a mistake." Scott sighed. "I just wish it hadn't been at my expense."

Matrice gave him a murderous look. "*Our* expense," she corrected. "In case you haven't noticed, I'm not exactly overjoyed at this development." She shaded her eyes as she looked out again, hoping against hope to catch a glimpse of her mother's boat returning. There was nothing to see but the ocean. She dropped her hand and turned toward Scott. She almost hated putting her next question into words. "How long do you think they'll leave us here?"

He shrugged. Right now, he knew he needed a few hours away from Valerie before he could trust himself to address her civilly again. But why did those hours have to be spent in the company of this rapier tongue with legs? "I don't know." He gave it some thought. "Until nightfall, I suppose."

Despite the warm climate, she shivered, running her hands up and down her arms. Hours. Hours alone with him. Talk about penance.

And what if it wasn't hours? What if it was longer?

Matrice glanced at the provisions Rita had left stacked on the beach while she'd naively been checking out the shack. Light filtered through the bottle of mouthwash, splintering and casting shimmering green and gold rainbows on the sand.

Mouthwash. Morning.

"Oh, God—" Matrice gasped as her hands flew to her mouth.

Scott looked around quickly, expecting to see some kind of creature, indigenous to the island, slithering out from somewhere. Instinctively, his hand flew out in a protective gesture, in spite of his feelings about Matrice.

"What? Where?" He didn't see a thing that hadn't been there before.

"I forgot about the mouthwash." She said the words accusingly, as if it was his fault.

"Mouthwash?" He echoed as he struggled to get his heart back under a hundred beats a minute. "You're giving me a heart attack over mouthwash?" he shouted, taking a threatening step toward her. The woman was a certifiable loon. "This isn't exactly the time to go overboard about personal hygiene."

Slapping the flat of her hand on his chest, she stopped him. Her palm stung, but she refrained from showing it. Just who the hell did he think he was, shouting at her?

"No. Don't you see, you idiot? If we were only going to be here a few hours, she wouldn't have left the mouthwash." Waving her hand at it without looking, her eyes blazed as they held his. "They're not coming back until morning." She dropped her hand, disheartened. "If then."

Scott groaned. "Of all the harebrained ideas..." His voice trailed off as several expletives occurred to him. He pressed his lips together to keep from voicing any of them. Damn. There was a brunch he was supposed to attend tomorrow at one. The Anderson account was riding on it. How the hell was he going to make it if he was stuck out here in the middle of the ocean with her?

Morning. She was stuck out here until morning. "Oh, Lord, I hope Mother feeds Travis."

"A sponging ex-boyfriend?" Scott guessed irritably. Maybe it *was* all a joke. Maybe Valerie would return within the hour, seeing the futility of all this.

No, Valerie wasn't coming, he decided. She was an optimist. She believed in happy endings. There'd be an ending in all this, all right. *His.* He was going to be tongue-lashed to death if he stayed here any length of time.

Matrice refused to even look at Scott. Why hadn't her mother packed a gun instead of a bottle of mouthwash?

"My dog," she informed him as she closed her eyes and sighed. She had to pull herself together and think. It would do no good to be angry at her mother now anyway. She'd save it for later, when she could do something about it. Revenge was going to be sweet. She sighed again, this time loudly, frustration clawing at her.

Scott looked at her. She seemed a little pale. He vaguely remembered Matrice saying something about not being able to endure hot weather. The conversation had involved the word *sweat*. He placed his hand on her arm. "You're not going to faint on me, are you?"

Matrice opened her eyes and jerked her arm away. He'd probably like that, having her crumple like a fragile female. "Not if you paid me."

He should have known concern would be wasted on someone like her. Vipers didn't need concern, they needed cages. "Sorry. For a second there, you looked pale. But I suppose that's just part of your standard house-haunting equipment."

She felt the slightest touch of guilt sweeping through her. The fact that Scott had momentarily displayed concern told her that perhaps, just perhaps, he was a modicum more human than she was giving him credit for.

At a loss, she shrugged helplessly. "Sorry, this situation has me a little uptight."

He hadn't expected an apology, not from her. "Too late. You've lost out on the Miss Congeniality award."

She let a small smile crease her lips. "Maybe next year."

Matrice shoved her hands into shallow pockets. She wished they were deeper. More than that, she wished she was home, in front of her television, watching this inane situation flicker across the screen instead of living it. At least then she'd be able to shut the set off.

Her skin was already beginning to tingle. She'd been out in the sun too long. Turning abruptly, she strode to where she had left her beach bag.

Curious, and because there wasn't anything else to do, Scott followed her. He watched as she dug into the depths of her purse. It resembled a small overnight bag.

"You wouldn't happen to have one of those little airline bottles of Scotch in there, would you?" He thought of the prospect of facing the next twenty-four hours with her. "Right about now, I think I could use a drink."

"No." She found the large bottle of aspirin she had thrown into her purse just in case another killer headache materialized. And it had. All six-foot-something of it. "If I did, I'd have first crack at it." Popping the cap with her thumb, she shook out two tablets. She downed them with half a cup of water from the bottled containers her mother had left behind.

She was tossing those tings into her mouth like candy, Scott thought. How many times had he seen that before? She probably didn't have enough sense to come in out of the rain, either. "Those things'll burn a hole in your stomach."

Dropping the aspirin into her purse, she searched for the suntan lotion bottle. Why was everything always on the bottom? "Thank you, Dr. diMarco, but I think I'll take care of my own stomach."

She didn't bother looking up at him, but hoped the remark annoyed him, just the way he annoyed her. The last thing she wanted was someone telling her what to do. No, she amended, the last thing she wanted was *him* telling her what to do.

Finally. She pulled the half empty plastic bottle of suntan lotion out and dropped the purse at her feet. If she didn't hurry, she was going to fry. Squeezing out a white glob of lotion into the palm of her hand, Matrice began to spread it slowly on her arms.

It was almost hypnotic, watching her apply the white cream along the curves of her body. Scott's eyes were drawn to the sight against his will. There was something primal, something sensuous about the caressing motion. He could vicariously feel the methodical stroke of her fingertips along his own skin, pressing, kneading, soothing. Arousing.

The screech of another sea gull made Scott blink and broke the trancelike state he had tumbled into. He reminded himself that the woman had the kind of personality that qualified her for first place in the Shrews Hall of Fame. Too bad. He had to admit that, at least physically, he found her very... appealing.

He took a deep breath, steadying his nerves. Twenty minutes was too soon to get island fever. And definitely much too soon to fall into the trap that Valerie and Matrice's mother had so blatantly laid out for him. Eternity would be too soon.

He was watching her. Without looking at him, she could feel his eyes on her. It made her feel unsure of herself. Uncomfortable. More than that, it unsettled her, nudging something unformed and sensual from within the depths of her consciousness.

The best defense, even against himself, was a strong offense. Scott launched into it. "If you're attempting to get yourself greased up so you'll slide out of my hands in case I try to make a grab for you, don't worry. I have absolutely no intentions of grabbing." He raised his hands, fingers up, toward the sky.

She stopped for a moment. Was he saying that because he was just insufferably annoying, or had the thought already crossed his mind? she suddenly wondered. The strange, tingling sensation within her intensified, even as she summoned her indignation against his disparaging dismissal of her.

She shook her head. "And Mother told me you had taste." She liberally applied the lotion to her bare midsection, aware that he was still watching her every move, like a wolf waiting to see a vulnerable spot open up within a flock of sheep. "For your information, I tend to burn when I'm out in the sun a lot. My skin's very fair."

Yes, he'd noticed. Fair, like freshly packed snow on the slopes of Mammoth in January. "That comes from never seeing the sun. Although I don't recall them ever having made up a lotion for moles."

Was that a crack about the hours she kept? Just how much information had her mother given to diMarco's sister-in-law? She highly resented being dissected by strangers. Especially *this* stranger.

"Thank God for you that a sense of humor is not a mandatory requirement for a stockbroker's license, or else you'd be selling hot dogs on the corner."

Having covered every square inch of her that she could reach, she now tried to cover the spots that weren't readily accessible to her. Her arms felt the strain as she reached over her shoulder.

He watched her struggle for a few moments, then decided she'd had enough. Even dumb animals shouldn't be left to chase their tail indefinitely. "How are you planning to do your back? Or are you double-jointed as well as fork-tongued?"

Out of patience, Matrice was about ready to throw the bottle at his head. "You would know about reptiles, wouldn't you?" She stretched her fingers and felt a cramp starting in her back. "Damn," she muttered. When he took the bottle from her, she could only stare. If he wanted some, why didn't he ask? Didn't the man have a single polite bone in his body? "What are you doing?"

For the first time since he'd found himself involuntarily stranded here, he grinned. "Basting you for the oven."

Squeezing a large glob into his hand, he slapped it on her back and began to rub—hard. Matrice winced and bit her lower lip to keep from crying out. He was doing this on purpose. She didn't want to give him the satisfaction of knowing that it hurt.

When the strokes became gentler, slower, Matrice had something else to deal with—her own involuntary responses. She clenched her hands at her sides, tensing even more.

Her back was smooth and soft to the touch, like creamy, expensive Italian leather. The more he touched her, the more he wanted to touch. He discovered, much to his annoyance, that he couldn't just divorce his thoughts from his actions. Undertaken through a purely selfish motive—a sunburned Matrice would undoubtedly be even more difficult to deal with than an unsunburned one—the process quickly became enjoyable. Sensual.

For an instant Scott let his mind drift as his emotions stirred. There was nothing else to do at this moment. Absolutely nothing. No telephones to answer, no clients to coddle, no reports to read. No crisis on the stock exchange to deal with. For all he knew right now, the rest of the world had just vanished. There was nothing to do but enjoy this.

His fingers swept along the slope of her back, dipping down her spine in even, languid strokes. He felt her involuntary shiver as he spread the thin cream to where the thin strap of her halter met her waist, and he heard her sharp intake of breath as his fingers discovered a highly sensitive point along her spine.

Matrice swallowed, fighting back a wave of what she knew had to be goose bumps attempting to form along her skin. Terrific. That was all she needed, for him to think he was giving her goose bumps. It was just the breeze, that was all. There *was* a breeze, wasn't there? Or was she just fervently hoping for one?

She felt her breath backing up in her lungs, stagnating in her chest as all sorts of odd sensations washed over her, wave after unsettling wave. Time to call a halt to this before it got out of hand.

"I think I'm well covered now." She swung around just as he was about to apply another palm full to her back. He wound up smearing it along the upper planes of her breasts instead.

Matrice jumped back as if he had just applied a hot poker to her skin. At least, it felt as if there was one burning in the center of her stomach.

"I think you're done," she told him in no uncertain terms, though her throat was quavering when she said it.

Though it had happened entirely by accident, Scott couldn't help the sudden, irresistible desire that rose within him to finish what fate had caused him to inadvertently start.

"Yes, I think I am." And then he grinned again. "You're dripping." His gaze moved down, indicating the point of their last contact.

Her eyes blazing, she dared him to take a step toward her as she rubbed the lotion into her skin quickly. She felt completely muddled inside. A dozen emotions tangled, grasping for control: anger, annoyance, frustration and a strange sense of anticipation. As if she was waiting for a storm to break.

Except that there wasn't a single cloud in the sky. The only storm in the vicinity seemed to be churning inside her.

He returned the suntan lotion to her. Matrice avoided his eyes and dropped the bottle into her purse. Scott tried not to stare at the inviting cleavage that was suddenly just a scant few inches away. Not having anything to do with her was going to be just a little harder than he'd thought.

Scott cleared his throat. "Why don't we see what Valerie and your mother left us in the way of provisions."

She already knew the answer to that. "My mother didn't leave any food. Just water. And mouthwash," she added distastefully.

That didn't sound right, but then, neither did leaving them stranded on an island together. It was getting so that you couldn't count on anyone these days. "Maybe they expect us to live on love."

"Don't hold your breath."

Matrice realized she'd literally snapped at him, but there was a reason for that. Self-preservation. She had reacted to him when he'd touched her, really reacted. And it worried her. She hadn't felt that kind of all-over, left-out-in-the-sun-melting feeling since the seventh grade. Then the feeling had been generated by a sexy movie star. Derek Reynolds had been an unattainable hunk of sexuality whose poster had graced the wall above her bed and who had, via daydreams, single-handedly nudged her into womanly awareness.

Matrice snuck a sidelong glance at the man at her side. In a way, Scott did resemble Derek Reynolds now that she thought of it. Especially around the mouth. It was full and sensual.

Oh, God, she thought with a sudden pang, she was in trouble here. Deep trouble. Wouldn't he think it was just hilarious if he knew that he reminded her of someone she had once had a mad crush on.

She pretended to gather together her meager provisions as she frowned to herself. She was going to have to do her best to keep him not at arm's length, but at whole body's length, as well.

She had an odd expression on her face as she looked at him, and wondered why. Well, they were stuck with one another and there had better be some ground rules, or at least some things cleared up.

"Look, the only thing I think we're in agreement on is surviving this and showing those two lovely, slightly addle-brained ladies that we are far from meant for each other. Agreed?" He put out his hand.

She hesitated for just a fraction of a second before placing her hand in his, as if loath to make any more contact with him than necessary. Why tempt the gods? "Agreed."

She was acting as if he had leprosy, he thought, curbing his annoyance. He was quick to let go of her hand. "Okay, now let's make the best of this situation. Valerie mentioned a shack."

"That's what it is, all right." She pointed off to his right. "It's that way."

He turned around. From here he could make out the very top. "Maybe they left something for us to eat there." The chest Val had left on the island earlier only contained bottles of water.

Matrice had already been there, but maybe she'd missed something in her quick perusal. At any rate, checking the shack for food would give them something to do for about a minute and a half. "All right, let's go."

Chapter Five

"It's a shack all right," Scott murmured as he walked across the grassy threshold just ahead of Matrice.

He moved slowly around the primitive ten-by-twelve structure, running his hand along the wall. They were just weather-beaten wooden planks nailed together. The roof was thatched, and the one window had no glass. The sun shone in through spaces between the blanking, attesting to both the quality of the material and the workmanship. It would afford them protection from the sun, but not much from the rain. The dirt floor was covered with some sort of leaves.

Scott shook his head in disbelief. It would be funny if it wasn't so serious. Or if he had someone else by his side instead of Matrice. "I feel as if we're on the set of a Tarzan movie."

Matrice moved aside just as something small, black and furry scurried across the floor and disappeared between the leaves. She desperately wanted her apartment and her nice, carpeted floor.

Her head snapped up at his comment. "Don't get any ideas. I am not Jane."

She wasn't his idea of Eve to his Adam, either. "The role of Cheetah is still being cast." He tested the walls for sturdiness and decided that he had been better off in his ignorance. They wobbled when he pushed against them. One strong gust and they'd go over. "Except, as I remember it," he turned to face her, "Cheetah had a fairly pleasant disposition."

She had had just about all she could take of his snide criticism. She went toe-to-toe with him, lifting her chin pugnaciously again. "And as I remember it, Tarzan was a big, dumb ape of a man."

He couldn't help laughing at her. She was almost cute when she was angry like this. A cute piranha, he amended. "Want to go a few rounds, Rocky?"

She supposed she was coming on a little strong at that, but he could get her so angry. Matrice backed off as gracefully as she could, given the circumstances. "Not in this heat. I'll take a rain check."

A glimmer of a sunbeam came in overhead and shone on the ground beneath his feet like a tiny spotlight. Scott looked up at the thatched roof. Through it he could see bits and pieces of the sky peeking out. "Not here, I hope. This place'll wash away in the first good rain."

She raised her eyes, concerned. She hadn't thought of that. What if it rained while they were here? "What's the weather forecast like?"

"For here?" he asked, incredulous that she expected him to know. "I haven't the slightest idea. It never occurred to me to listen for forecasts for deserted islands off Nantucket when I live in New York."

He was being sarcastic again. When would she learn not to ask him questions and expect a decent answer? Matrice moved to the other end of the shack, though that didn't provide much distance from him.

"If anything, this calls to mind Robinson Crusoe and his man, Friday," she told him.

He frowned. Leave it to her to cast him in a subservient role. "I suppose you want me to be Friday."

She smiled. "My last name is Crusoe. By process of elimination, that makes you Friday."

"We'll negotiate," he muttered.

There was a small table and two chairs standing in one corner. Matrice ran her hand over the table. No dust. Her mother probably had it brought over yesterday. How long had the woman been plotting this?

Matrice glanced over toward Scott. He was examining the pile of supplies that had been left behind for them. There was a frying pan, two plates, a couple of cooking utensils, matches, firewood and a single sleeping bag.

He gave a short, disparaging laugh under his breath as he held up the latter for her benefit. "Not very subtle, are they?"

She tried not to cringe. *I'll get you for this, Mother.* Matrice shoved her hands into her pockets, clenching them at her sides. "Who gets the sleeping bag?"

He shrugged. That wasn't his main concern at the moment. "Whoever needs it the most at the end of the day."

Scott turned the sleeping bag over, thinking that perhaps he had missed something. He hadn't. Rising, he threw his hands up in disgust. This was unbelievable.

"There's no food," he announced in amazement. He kicked aside something that resembled a spear, annoyed. Fun was fun, but this was going too far. "How could they leave us with no food?"

Matrice looked down at the metal rod Scott had kicked out of his way. She should have known. With a smile, she bent down and picked it up.

Scott eyed the spear with a genuine healthy respect as Matrice wrapped her fingers around it. From the way she held it, he knew she wasn't unfamiliar with the weapon. "What do you intend to do with that?"

A cryptic remark was on the tip of her tongue, but she let it pass. The spear had a nice balance to it, she thought, weighing it thoughtfully on her palm. "This is for our dinner."

He thought it prudent to remain where he was. No sense tempting her. That thing did look sharp. "A little sparse, don't you think? Isn't there supposed to be something skewered on the end of it?" *Preferably not me.*

Her mother had provided two of them, she realized. The other was peeking out from beneath the frying pan. She bent over to reach for it.

"Yes, a fish. As in do-it-yourself." She couldn't help the grin that came to her lips. "Think fast, diMarco." With the ease of someone who knew their way around hunting equipment, Matrice tossed the spear to him, rounded end first.

Surprised and definitely not in his element, Scott made a grab for the spear and dropped it. He hopped out of the way as the tip fell near his foot. He gave her a black look. "I am thinking fast, and you wouldn't like what I'm thinking."

Maybe it would be better to get some time away from him. "All right, just as well. Stay here and I'll catch dinner." Turning her back on him, she walked outside.

He wasn't a chauvinist, he told himself. He really wasn't. But he also wasn't about to let her get one up on him, either. Picking up the spear, Scott hurried after her. As he moved, the spear felt awkward in his hand, as if it didn't belong there.

He eased his stride as he caught up to her. "You really know how to use one of those things?"

She looked over her shoulder, not bothering to hide her superior smile. "Yes."

Her smug demeanor rankled him and his next comment was voiced automatically. "Is that how you convinced Marlow to change firms? By pointing a spear at him?"

Matrice stopped wading into the water and turned, her fingers tightening about her spear. She had been competing in a man's world ever since she came to work on Wall Street. She'd had to work twice as hard to gain every inch up the ladder as any man in her firm and resented Scott's flippant remark more than he dreamed possible.

Eyes flashing, hair tangled and unruly, she reminded him of a drawing of an Amazon, the magnificent kind. He erased the thought from his mind.

"I'd watch what I said to a woman with a spear in her hand if I were you," she warned.

He inclined his head, pretending to bow and humor her. "Yes, ma'am."

The breeze ruffled her hair and she pushed it out of her eyes, wishing she had something to secure it with besides a ribbon. "Better." She turned and looked around at the waters. At least her mother had chosen a place where the fishing was good, she thought. Like the table, that, too, was no doubt by design. Her mother might look vague, but there was a sharp mind at work in that head of hers. "Now, if you'd like a lesson, come on in. Otherwise—" she waved a hand in the direction of the shack "—find something to do and make yourself useful."

She was hoping he'd pick the latter choice, but he waded into the water and stopped a foot away from her. "I think I'll save hide tanning for tomorrow, Crusoe." The smile on his lips was easy and his words were without an edge. It was a nice change, she thought.

She felt herself grinning. "You are a disappointment to me, Friday. You surely are." A little of her own tension, as well as most of her anger, was abating. There was nothing she could do about the situation she found herself in at the moment, so she might as well just go along with it.

Having the spear in her hand brought back a lot of old, fond memories for her. She was twelve again. Within her mind, she could almost hear her father's deep, baritone voice patiently instructing her as he stood beside her in the brilliantly clear Florida waters, his hand over hers, his keen instincts seeming to flow into her as he spoke.

Scott looked around, surprised to see fish swimming in the same area as he was standing. He jumped as he felt something bump up against the back of his leg. When he looked down, a blur of green and blue was darting away from him. He threw the spear after it and missed the mark by a wide margin.

Matrice sucked in her breath. That wild throw could just as easily have been in her direction. "Careful, you'll scare the fish." *Not to mention maim me.*

Muttering, he retrieved his spear. "What about the fish scaring me?"

Retracing his steps toward her, Scott looked around uncertainly. Another fish darted by, almost between his legs. He reacted too late and didn't even both to attempt to spear it. This was definitely not his element. He was a city boy, born and bred. The closest he had ever come to wildlife was skirting the perimeter of Central Park at twilight.

He looked up to see Matrice watching him, an amused smile on her lips. "What?" he demanded.

Matrice looked down into the waters again. Obviously it was up to her to get dinner. "I take it you've never fished before?"

He felt like a fool and dropped his hand to his side, retiring the spear. "You mean with a rod and reel, or like Hiawatha?"

"Either." With a little exclamation of triumph, she secured the entrée to their evening meal. She pulled the fish from the spear and tossed it onto the beach, then looked at Scott, waiting for an answer.

There was no point in lying. She could see for herself that he wasn't any good at this. "No."

Scott watched with a touch of envy as Matrice quickly aimed and threw her spear straight down into the water in less time than it took him to draw a breath. He hated to admit it, but she was good. "How did you learn to do that?"

She tossed the second fish next to the first on the beach. Cautiously, she moved to another section, then waited, poised. "My dad. He used to take me spear fishing off the coast of Florida every summer."

The fond note in her voice caught his attention. Her face softened as she spoke. For a moment, she looked gentle. The contrast was almost laughable, considering the lethal spear in her hand.

When he made no comment, Matrice raised her eyes to find him studying her again. The same fluttering, uneasy feeling occurred. She didn't like the silence, not with him. "What did you do with your father?"

"Nothing."

His answer begged for a sarcastic retort, yet something stopped her. Though his face was impassive, there'd been a hint of sorrow, or regret perhaps, in Scott's voice as he'd said the single word. Matrice raised her hair from her neck, let the breeze cool it, then allowed the chestnut mass to fall back. "Oh."

Scott looked off into the horizon. Sunlight was dancing on the water, scattering about like fairies in rainbow costumes. "He died when I was twelve. Car accident. My mother was with him."

She felt awful, as if she had just willfully tramped through sacred ground with cleats on. But it hadn't been on purpose. Her mother hadn't said anything about his parents being dead. "Oh, Scott, I'm so sorry. I didn't know."

He shrugged. A hint of an ironic smile twisted his lips. The spear in his hand was totally forgotten. "He was an airline pilot. Flew I don't know how many times cross-country. Fifteen years. Never even a near miss. No problems, nothing." Unconsciously, he turned toward Matrice, as if needing the comfort of her eyes. "They were killed by a drunk driver while going to celebrate their twenty-first anniversary." The smile that continued to curve his lips was without mirth. "I guess twenty-one was their unlucky number."

Scott realized that she had stopped fishing, the spear still poised in her hand. A fish swam right by her and she didn't notice. She was too busy listening to him. He didn't want the pity he saw in her eyes. He liked her better when she was throwing barbs at him.

He pointed to the water. "You let the fish get away," he muttered.

"There'll be others." Her voice was raspy. She cleared her throat. There was a lump in it as she envisioned the orphaned young boy he had been.

She could see that her sympathy made him uncomfortable. Looking for a way to change the subject, she nodded toward the water. "Why don't you try your luck again?"

He didn't know what had come over him. He usually didn't talk about his parents. He certainly didn't want her sympathy. Scott looked around. He also didn't relish the idea of trying—and failing—again around her. "I don't like piercing fish."

She saw through his lie and smiled. "You like being hungry better?"

No, but he liked being shown up even less. Scott cast about for a way out and made a calculated guess. "Do you know how to cook?"

The smoke alarm in her kitchen went off with regularity. She stiffened slightly. "Is this an interview?"

The ball, he knew, had just been successfully lobbed back into her court. "Then you don't, do you?"

She wasn't about to give him an opportunity to gloat. And to think, a moment ago, she was feeling sorry for him! She should have her head examined.

"I'm alive, aren't I?" She looked down at the water. Where had the fish gone? She moved to another spot, careful not to create any waves. "That would mean that somewhere along the line, I've had to have cooked something."

Not necessarily. "If you could cook, you'd be rubbing my nose in it."

He had her there, she thought, but she wasn't about to tell him so. "I can cook well enough, thank you."

He grinned. He was a fair hand at cooking. Valerie had taught him early and well. He had worked his way through college preparing meals in the kitchen of a hotel restaurant. "I can probably cook better."

Matrice forgot about fishing and lifted a brow as she studied what she saw as his arrogant profile. "Are we going to go through all the choruses of 'Anything You Can Do,' or just hum the refrain?"

The man who wound up with this woman as his wife had Scott's wholehearted pity. "Neither. What I'm going for is a division of labor."

So far, she was doing all the laboring. Matrice turned her attention back to fishing. "If you're always so direct, no wonder you lost the Marlow account."

Was she going to bring that up every time they had a conversation? "Can we just drop the Marlow account while we're stuck out here?"

A glimmer of color caught her attention and she raised the spear, eyes trained on the water. "You were the one who brought it up last."

Scott studied her throat and wondered if he was bound by U.S. law while stranded out here. He pressed on. "My point is that you seem to be able to fish better than I can—"

Matrice looked up. "Seem?"

He ignored the offended tone. "—and I can probably cook a hell of a lot better than you."

Damn, she had just let another fish get away. "I'll reserve judgment on that."

He watched a large fish swim right by her, aware and pleased that he had distracted her. "So you catch, I'll cook."

"Okay, deal—as long as you—" she threw the spear and grinned with satisfaction as she caught another fish "—clean them in the bargain."

He didn't like the idea of her getting the last word in. "You do the dishes."

The fish was large and she had some difficulty getting it off the end of the spear. "Maybe you should have been a lawyer."

Part of him would have been content watching her struggle, but some things were just too ingrained to ignore. With a sigh, he took the spear from her and pulled the fish off, throwing it next to the others. It was shaping up to be quite a meal after all. "Is that a yes?"

"Thanks," she said grudgingly, nodding at the latest addition to the catch. She sighed, knowing he was waiting for an answer. She supposed it was only fair. "All right, that's a yes."

Life was made up of victories. Some of them were tiny, but significant nonetheless. This was one of them. "And here I thought you only stopped arguing when you were asleep."

She took her spear back and moved farther away. The waves lapped at the back of her legs, soaking the edge of her shorts. Why hadn't she packed a second pair? she thought irritably. Simple. Because she hadn't expected to be stranded her with George of the Jungle, that's why. "If that's part of your charm, no wonder you're still not married."

About to pick up the pile of fish, he stopped. The woman never missed an opportunity. "What's your excuse?"

She had expected as much. "I already told you, I'm too busy. There are too many frogs out there to kiss while trying to find a prince." She glanced in his direction when she said the word *frogs*.

He decided to leave the fish where they were for the time being and sat down on the sand. He clasped his hands around his legs and watched the way the sun played off her hair, weaving red highlights through it. "Did you ever stop to think that maybe you just scared them away and they couldn't turn into princes?"

"Are you saying I'm intimidating?" She didn't like the image that conjured up in her mind. She wasn't intimidating, she thought. She'd even had proposals, but she wasn't about to tell *him* that. It was just that there was always something wrong with the man doing the proposing and she wasn't inclined to be hasty about making a lifelong commitment.

He laughed. "Well, you're no shrinking violet."

She grew defensive. Who was he to judge her, anyway? "If I was, I wouldn't be on Wall Street."

Out of the corner of his eye, he saw a sea gull circling and wondered if he was going to have to defend their dinner. "Is that where you want to be? On Wall Street?"

For a second she tried to concentrate on the way the waves felt against her body and not on what he was saying to her. She didn't like being analyzed and she could hear it coming. "Yes."

"Why?"

Did he think the territory belonged solely to people who buttoned their jackets from left to right? "For the same reason you probably do. It's exciting."

She said that a little too fiercely to convince him. He wondered if she was in the same sort of rut a lot of people he knew were. Running with the pack because they were afraid of what they'd find was out there if they stopped. "When I'm excited, I don't swallow aspirin. That was the jumbo-size bottle you were carrying. Just how large a headache were you expecting to get in just a few hours?"

"Not as large as the one I got." She looked at him pointedly.

The sea gull flew away and Scott relaxed. He leaned back on his elbows and watched her in silence. There was something seductively poetic about the way she was standing there, legs spread apart, hardly moving, waiting. Artemis, the goddess of the hunt. Too bad she was more like Medusa.

Maybe that was all the fish they were going to get today, she thought. She glanced toward the beach. Scott looked like he was about to fall asleep. "This too strenuous for you?"

He grinned. He couldn't remember the last time he'd actually kicked back and relaxed this way, other than grabbing a few hours at Val and Frank's every Sunday. But even then, he had never felt lazy. And there was always something to hurry off to looming just ahead. He had nowhere to hurry to here. "No, actually, I'm having less difficulty doing this than I'd have thought."

"What?" He was going to make some kind of crack about her not being as hard on the eyes as he'd thought, she just knew it.

"Relaxing." A warm, southerly breeze was picking up and it caressed his body, reinforcing the hypnotic effect created by the sun. "At home, I don't seem to know how to relax. It always feels as if I should be doing something productive with my time, as if every minute is being wasted if I'm not accomplishing something."

She could relate to that. "Like now."

The breeze ruffled his hair. His first inclination was to smooth it back down, but he let it go. There didn't seem to be a point. "No, right now you're getting dinner."

"And you?"

He stretched out. The sand felt warm and seductive against the back of his legs. "I'm watching you get dinner."

"Very productive." She tired to summon a shaft of sarcasm, but found herself depleted, at least for the moment.

Obviously she was not in the right frame of mind to relax yet. "This isn't something that can be put on a flow chart or tracked on the market."

She conjured up the image in her mind and laughed. "No, it's not."

He was surprised, but her laugh pleased him. "That's nice."

"What is?"

"Your laugh." It was sexy, making him think of balmy summer nights with a blanket of stars overhead and the scent of carnations from his planter filling the air. "When it isn't aimed at me."

She speared a small fish, then eyed the collection on the shore. Maybe that was enough for now. "How hungry are you?"

The water reflected the sunlight, making it glimmer and sparkle all around her as it danced on the surface. For a woman who barely came up to his shoulder, she gave the appearance of having long, clean lines. He felt something stirring within the center of his stomach. It had nothing to do with food.

"Very," he murmured, then realized what he had just said. He wasn't talking about dinner. He had to stop letting his mind drift like that. He knew what she was like. Just because they were out here didn't change anything. They were as compatible as bulls and bears on the stock-market floor.

Stupid, that's what it was, Matrice chastised herself. Why should that one word feel as if it were skimming along her skin like a warm caress, working its way through her defenses into her very core? He was talking about fish, about dinner, not her.

Besides, if he made one wrong move toward her, she was going to find another use for this spear. She wasn't about to let him take advantage of the situation or her, not after all the things he'd said to her and all the things he'd implied.

"Does this look like enough to you, or do you want me to catch more?" She enunciated each word slowly, between clenched teeth.

He needed to put some distance between them. He was fantasizing about a female shark. "One more for luck." Scott rose to his feet. Tiny grains of sand rained down from his legs as he leaned over to pick up the fish. "I'd better get started on these. Did you happen to see a knife in our survival kit? I'd hate to have to gut these things with my teeth."

"Lovely image. I think you'll find one next to the frying pan."

He nodded and took their dinner back to the hut.

Alone, she let herself relax again. Odd, how nervous he made her, considering the fact that she didn't even like the man.

It was another ten minutes before she caught the last fish. Satisfied, she picked up both spears as well as the fish and returned to the shack.

When she saw him, Scott was sitting cross-legged outside the hut, gutting a fish on a rock. With his bronzed skin and dark hair, he looked like a native from one of the South Pacific Islands. She'd been meaning to take a trip there one of these years, if she ever found the time. Now it seemed as if the island had found her instead.

His muscles rippled as he worked at cleaning the fish. She felt her breath growing short and decided she had been out in the water too long.

Feeling her presence, Scott looked up, waiting for her to say something.

"I brought you one more." She held it out awkwardly. He was evaporating her self-assurance in the space of one afternoon.

He nodded toward the fish he hadn't cleaned yet. "Put it down there."

She dropped it on the pile. "How come you're out here? Wouldn't the table be easier?" Not to mention a little cooler, out of the sun, she thought, then remembered that he had said the heat didn't bother him.

"I don't want the shack to smell of fish. After all—" his gaze reached up the length of her body "—we'll have to sleep there."

She could almost feel him touching her and she shivered. Her throat felt dry. She looked past Scott into the shack. The single sleeping bag was just in view. "Yes, I guess we will." This was ridiculous. She was a grown woman. Besides, he wasn't about to pounce on her. What was there to be afraid of?

She took a deep breath, as if that would fortify her against the direction her mind was going. "Do you need any help with that?"

He shook his head, skillfully filleting the fish. "No, it's your turn to relax."

She dragged a hand through her hair and the ribbon came undone. It floated to the grass a few feet away. She stooped down to pick it up. "I don't think I know how," she admitted.

He wished she'd stop bending over that way in front of him. Willpower only went so far, even when it involved a shrew.

Scott indicated the ground with the tip of his knife. "Start out by sitting down. The sun'll do the rest."

Matrice glanced up mechanically. "The sun," she muttered, as if suddenly aware of it for the first time. She'd been standing in saltwater for a while. The suntan lotion had probably long since washed away. "I'd better put more lotion on my legs. Otherwise, they'll be bright red before I get a chance to sample your great culinary skills."

He was oblivious to her parting shot as a sensation returned to him—the sensation he'd experienced rubbing suntan lotion on her back. He glanced over his shoulder at her as she went into the hut. "Need any help?"

She stopped and looked at him oddly. "Putting lotion on my legs?"

"Never mind." That was a slip. He had better keep his mind on his work, he thought, and not on the way her hand, even now, was slowly sliding up her legs as she rubbed the lotion in.

Scott stifled a yelp as he accidentally pricked his finger with the knife. The woman even managed to draw blood by proxy.

Chapter Six

"Well?" Scott finally asked.

She had been eating now for several minutes. In that time she hadn't said a single word, or given any indication that she was enjoying the meal. The stoneware dish was almost empty.

Matrice raised her eyes to his. Something inside her stubbornly resisted giving him his due. "I've had better."

Scott sighed. He might have known she wouldn't concede the matter. "At least you're not claiming I poisoned you. I guess that's something."

There was stubborn and then there was pigheaded, and Matrice knew when she had crossed the line. She ran the tip of her tongue along her lips as she stared into the fire's flames. She could give him a compliment, but she didn't have to look at him when she did it.

"Somewhere," she added quietly. She was aware that Scott had stopped eating and was looking at her in astonishment. Then a pleased smile began to creep across his lips.

She tried not to react to it, even though it was disarming. "I must have had better at some point somewhere. But this is very good."

The filleted fish was so soft, so tender, it practically melted on her tongue before she had a chance to chew it. "How did you manage to make it taste so good?" She gestured toward the hut. The supplies that had been left behind for them were nominal. "You had nothing to work with."

The satisfied grin spread over his entire face. "Skill."

That didn't begin to answer her question. "Even skill needs seasonings," she persisted.

He raised a brow, his eyes skimming over her. She sat near him, her legs tucked under her small rear. The light from the camp fire made her pale skin gleam like gold found in the arc of a rainbow after a spring shower. He moved back a little. The fire seemed to be getting a little too warm for him.

"Not always. Sometimes it's just knowing when, knowing how. Anticipating," he paused for a beat before adding, "the right temperatures."

Why did she have the feeling that he wasn't really talking about cooking? She had the distinct impression that it was her in the frying pan now instead of the last of their dinner.

With conscious effort, she drew her eyes away from his mouth. Island madness she supposed they'd call it. Though she held all handsome men suspect because of the shallowness she'd encountered, Matrice couldn't deny the fact that she felt really attracted to Scott. It had to be the circumstances. It certainly couldn't be the man himself, even if he could cook better than anyone she had ever met.

The light from the fire played on the planes of her shoulders, making them appear soft, inviting. He looked down at her plate. It was safer that way. "Would you like more?"

"Please." She cleared her throat self-consciously, realizing that she sounded as if she were begging for something other than another serving of grilled fish. Above everything else, she didn't want him getting the impression that she was attracted to him.

Matrice looked at the piece of fish as he placed it on her plate. The man was good. If he could work miracles using nothing, what could he do with a whole spice rack at his disposal? No longer ravenous, she still enjoyed the meal. "If you ever get tossed out of Wall Street, you could always become a chef. Seriously, why didn't you become a chef?"

He shrugged. Sometimes he wondered about that himself. He explored the feelings out loud, surprising himself. It wasn't his habit to expose his private thoughts. "I guess I didn't want to ruin it by bringing money into it. Cooking's my hobby. It relaxes me." He wondered if she'd laugh at that.

She didn't laugh, but she did shake her head, her hair sweeping along her shoulders like a veil made of dusk and dreams. He wanted to reach out and touch it.

"Not me. Turning on the oven always makes me nervous." She was completely hopeless in the kitchen. Her mother had once commented that she was the only person Rita knew who could burn water. "You were right, I can't really cook."

Finishing the last of her meal, she placed the empty plate down on the ground next to her and drew her legs up, crossing her arms over them. She felt sated. "My idea of survival is living near a good restaurant that delivers to a few valued customers."

Scott had had his fill of restaurants from the other end while going to school. And he had seen enough going on in the kitchen to make him leery of dining out for pleasure. He could whip up anything that could be found in a high-quality restaurant.

"Something else we don't have in common," he noted. "I don't really care to eat in restaurants, unless I'm doing business."

She remembered their first encounter. She turned her head and looked at him suspiciously. "But you suggested meeting me in a restaurant."

There was one piece of fish left in the frying pan, but he was too full. To set his plate on top of hers, he had to reach over her. Their arms brushed against one another. Scott moved back carefully, not entirely pleased with what he was feeling. "My point exactly."

Why was she attracted to someone like this? Maybe she was coming unglued and didn't know it. "You consider marriage coming under the heading of business?"

"Of a sort." Her silence, he thought, was ominous, but he pressed on, cataloguing it for her. "Finding the right person, making certain you have common backgrounds, common interests. Good genes. Everything that would be involved in making a good business move." He tried to make it as sterile-sounding as possible, though he wasn't feeling very sterile or antiseptic at the moment.

Those had actually been her sentiments at the time, but hearing Scott say them out loud made it all sound so cold, so detached. So depressingly lifeless. She decided that it went with his image. "When they start making clones, you should really be in your element."

He didn't care for her snide tone. "Oh, and you came to meet me geared up for romance?"

No, she hadn't. At least not when she'd walked through the restaurant door. But one meeting with him had her hungering for it, because he had seemed so devoid of the quality. "Yes, in a way."

He stared at her. Was she serious? He remembered the impression he'd gotten of her after just a few words had been exchanged, mostly hers. She exuded the total antithesis of romance. "In what way? Was I supposed to sweep you off your feet along with the check?"

She grasped the frying pan handle to move the pan next to the plates. "Checks don't have feet and you wouldn't know romance if it hit you in the head."

He eyed the frying pan she was still holding. "Is that a threat?"

She frowned, letting the pan drop. "That is an observation." She dusted off her hands, as if that would dust him from her life, as well. "I have no idea what Mother and your sister-in-law were thinking of, trying to get us together."

Why did that statement annoy him so much? It was exactly what he thought, too. Did he just have an inclination to say "day" when she said "night," or was there something else going on here? No, he didn't want to delve too deeply into this. He was afraid of what he might find.

"There, at least we agree." He rose to his feet, glancing at the sky as he did.

The moon was big and full and made for romance. Now where the hell had that come from? Some old song he had once heard? He crossed his arms and stared off toward the ocean. From here it looked black, with a shimmering golden stairway running straight across it and up toward the moon.

There would be no romance tonight, not with the likes of her. "Despite what I gather are similar backgrounds and careers, you and I are simply just not suited for one another."

An infinitesimal twinge of sorrow pricked her at his words. "Nope," she agreed. She felt oddly empty and alone as she said it.

He didn't care for the way she agreed so easily, ready to write him off. Not when he couldn't do the same so readily. "I mean, there's just no chemistry, no fire. Anyone could see that." The words rang a little hollow to his ear, but he said them anyway.

Matrice glared up at him, then scrambled to her feet. She had tried to be nice, complimenting him on his cooking. Weren't his insults ever going to stop? No, of course not. He was just a typical, smug male. "Oh, they could, could they?"

What was she getting so worked up about? He was just agreeing with her initial statement. "Yes."

"Well, it's not my fault."

He dropped his hands to his sides as he slowly turned toward her. Where did she get off, casting aspersions at him? "Are you insinuating that it's mine?"

She hadn't been the cold fish at the restaurant. That honor had belonged to him. *She* had arrived ready to be friendly. "Well, isn't it?"

He moved closer to her. Close enough to smell the shampoo she used in her hair, the soap she used on her body. He could feel something tightening, waiting, a compressed spring ready to release its energy at the slightest provocation. "How do you know that?"

The look in his eyes had alarms going off in her head, but she pushed on anyway. "I thought it was 'obvious,' remember?" She was angry at him, at the way he was making her react when he couldn't care less. "Besides, it's something one assumes about cold fish."

He drew himself up. In the moonlight, he made her think of a marble statue of some forgotten god. "I'm Italian," he said with equal parts of umbrage and passion. "There's nothing cold about me."

Fire, she was playing with fire, fire far more dangerous than the one within the circle of rocks at their feet. "I'd say put your money where your mouth is, but—"

Matrice got no further in her challenge. Scott angrily pulled her into his arms. The air flew out of her as his chest came in contact with hers.

She had goaded him. Knowingly, willingly, she had goaded him into this. She *wanted* him to kiss her. Whether it was to prove to herself that there wasn't anything there between them, that it was all just her imagination, or to show him exactly what he was missing by being the snob he was, she wasn't certain. She just knew she *had* to kiss him. But the first move had to be his.

And the final word had to be hers.

She consciously pulled out all the stops and placed everything she had into that one kiss. Letting go of the rein she always tightly kept on her passions, forgetting about consequences, remembering only that she had to show this egotistical man that what he was so easily dismissing was something he should be eternally grateful for finding, Matrice poured her entire soul into this single meeting of lips.

Her mouth hungrily slid over his, igniting, stoking, feeding. She set a trap and heard it snap shut. Behind her.

No passion? He'd show her no passion. If there was anything he knew he was, it was passionate. It was just that passion had no place in his day-to-day life. It had been sitting on the shelf, gathering intensity. It slipped off the shelf now.

And exploded on contact.

If he was a cold fish, why was she the one who was suddenly hooked? Matrice thought with mounting desperation. The hunter had somehow become the hunted. She could have sworn the ground shook beneath her feet. Maybe the island was sinking. Maybe she was.

Their lips met with a thunderclap of intensity that left her weak and shaken. Held tightly against his chest, she could do nothing but stay there. If he let go, she knew she would slide right down to the ground, completely boneless.

Damn him, it wasn't supposed to be this way.

Summoning strength from somewhere, Matrice returned a second volley, wrapping her arms around his neck and pressing herself even closer against him than she already was. The heat rose between them, sizzling and crackling like high-intensity power lines on a misty morning.

If no chemistry existed, then why was the entire laboratory suddenly exploding on him? Scott was rocked by surprise and utter disbelief. Begun in anger, the kiss had mushroomed, growing a thousandfold until it ensnared not only her senses—he hoped—but his own, as well. Hopelessly so.

He slanted his mouth over hers, again and again, drinking in the sweet taste of her lips, her breath tantalizing him. He felt her heart hammering wildly beneath the thin material of her halter. He longed to get rid of the flimsy barrier.

He didn't want it to stop here. He wanted it to continue. He wanted, more than anything else, to make love with her. The realization shocked him, hitting like a sudden summer shower that came from nowhere without a single warning.

No, there had been warnings. If he was honest with himself, there had been warning signs. He had just denied them, not wanting it to be true. It made no sense. She hated him and he couldn't abide her.

And yet he wanted her.

He wanted her in his bed, wanted her beneath him, crying out his name, giving of herself. He wanted to make love with her until he was too exhausted to care that he was marooned on a godforsaken island with a woman who thought he gave cold fish a bad name.

His body heated to almost unbearable levels as he ran his hands along her back, the smooth, bare planes stirring his blood, his fantasies.

Damn, he wished it was someone else doing this to him instead of her. Anyone else.

All he knew was that he wanted her. Now.

Somewhere, on a faraway plane, Matrice thought she felt the sides of her halter loosening. She had to stop now, before there was no turning back. If she gave in to herself, gave in to this enormous, formless craving that was seizing her and made love with him, he'd only laugh at her when it was over. He'd probably yell out something like, "April fool," even though it was the end of August. And the only part of it that would be right would be the word *fool*.

Struggling, not wanting to stop this any more than she wanted to stop breathing, Matrice managed to wedge her hands between them. With the last bit of strength she had, she pushed on the hard, rigid surface that he called a chest. It probably matched his heart, she thought with a pang.

He looked at her in puzzled disorientation, like someone just sliding off a wild, spinning ride in an amusement park. She felt frazzled, dazed and almost entirely desolate that it had to stop here, even though she knew it did. That was her mind talking. Her body was begging her to go on.

She had to wait until her heart stopped pounding in her throat before she could utter a word. "Just like you said." She pulled more air into her lungs before continuing. "There is no chemistry."

The hell there wasn't and she knew it. He wanted to shout at her for doing this to him, for tangling him up this way. He had never been attracted to a woman in this wild, mindless way before. Never been in a situation where his control had nearly broken away from him. When he was with a woman, there had always been a conscious progression of events. And he had always seen it all happening clearly: the intimate melding of bodies, the entwining of limbs. It had always been as if he were hovering just above, watching. But this time he wasn't watching. He was too involved to be aware of anything but his own raw needs.

"No," he agreed, his voice almost a whisper along her skin. "None."

She was going to suffocate if she didn't take in another deep gulp of air. Turning from him, trying not to be obvious, she dragged in another lungful of air. Her pulse was still tap-dancing. "I guess we're agreed then."

"Yes, we are." *No, we're not. I don't think I even know my name right now.*

She dragged a hand through her hair, wishing her skin would cool off. She moved away from the fire and went into the hut. Moonlight was shining in through the doorway and the window. It made her feel lonely.

She needed to get some rest before she weakened and did something she knew she'd regret for the rest of her life. She licked her lips. They felt tread worn. "I'll toss you for the sleeping bag."

He began to throw dirt on the fire. It hissed and groaned in protest as the flames died. There was no point in staying up, he thought, not when there was only one thing he wanted to do. One very foolish thing.

He glanced at the small stack by the side of the camp fire. "What about the dishes?"

She was suddenly bone weary. "They can make their own arrangements."

He rose, brushing the dirt from his hands. "I meant, what about washing them? Our agreement, remember?"

She couldn't remember anything except the way his mouth had felt against hers, the way his body had leaned into her own. "Tomorrow," she promised. "I'll do it to-morrow." *When I can walk to the ocean.*

He walked in behind her. Their shadows melded on the wall and became one. She felt an ache threatening to over-take her. *Steady, Matrice, remember how the man feels about you.*

Scott looked at the lone sleeping bag in the center of the hut. He spoke before he could stop himself. "You know, it's is large enough for—"

She swung around, her eyes blazing. Her hand darted out and she pushed hard against his chest. It was a symbolic, futile gesture. "Don't even think it." Why did she sud-denly feel like crying?

She looked upset. Maybe she wasn't as immune to what had just happened as he'd thought she was. He shrugged, attempting to be nonchalant when all he wanted to do was kiss her again. "All right, then you take it."

She looked at him, expecting there to be a condition at-tached to his offer. When he didn't add anything, she could only murmur, "Thank you." Like a kite string that sud-denly snapped in a strong April wind, she collapsed onto the sleeping bag.

It was a warm night, but she burrowed into the sleeping bag, vainly attempting to cocoon herself away from him, away from her own feelings.

Him, why did it have to be him? Of all the men in the world, why did she have to feel something for a man who detested her? It didn't seem fair. She was so wrapped up in her immediate situation, she didn't even realize that for the first time in her life, she wasn't running for the hills at the first sign of emotional commitment. She was looking for it.

Scott took off his T-shirt and bunched it up as best he could, then placed it beneath his head. Arms folded akimbo, he lay on his back and stared at the beams of moonlight filtering through the spaces in the roof. He damned the woman next to him for existing. Every inch of his body was aware of the fact that she was there.

And he was here.

He supposed that was where the expression, so near and yet so far, had originated from, a situation exactly like this one. He knew the blame for all this ultimately lay with him. If he had only cut Valerie off at the beginning, he wouldn't be lying here in the dark, frustrated, wanting a woman who despised the ground he walked on and took delight in showing him up at every turn.

Knowing didn't make it any easier to accept. Scott lay awake for a long time.

Sea gulls screeching to one another overhead woke him the next morning to a painful awareness. He felt stiff all over. Something else to blame on Matrice, he thought irritably. It wasn't actually her fault that they were stranded out here, but he had to blame someone and she was the best candidate he had.

To his annoyance, his restless night hadn't done anything to abate his desire, or improve his mood. If anything, both were worse.

Scott dragged his hand slowly over his face. God, he hoped that Valerie would return for him today. He didn't know how much more of this he could take. Rolling over, he looked in Matrice's direction.

The sleeping bag was empty.

He jackknifed into a sitting position and regretted it instantly. Spasms were telegraphing his back's displeasure over the night he had just spent.

"Matrice?" he called. There was no response, except for the sea gulls. Damn it, where was she?

He listened for her, but couldn't hear anything. Even the sea gulls had stopped. What if the boat had arrived early this morning? Would she have gone off and left him? She had seemed awfully upset last night.

No, even she wouldn't be that inhuman. He was being ridiculous. Rather than relax him, his enforced stay on this so-called island paradise had him edgy. No, he amended, *she* had him edgy.

He rose and called her name again. There was still no answer. Maybe she was in trouble. Maybe the island wasn't uninhabited the way they'd thought.

Concerned, angry, he rushed out of the hut and looked around. She was nowhere to be seen. Adrenaline began to pump through him.

"Damn it, Matrice, this isn't funny. Where the hell are you?" Shading his eyes, Scott squinted, scanning the area. Where was Valerie, for God's sake? Why wasn't she here? And above all, where was that viper-tongued woman?

Not being able to think of anything else, he headed for the beach where they had been fishing yesterday. Where *she* had been fishing, he corrected himself. Maybe she was just getting fish for their breakfast, or washing off the plates and frying pan. In his hurry, he hadn't noticed if they were gone.

If he found her and she was all right, he was going to kill her.

A tiny scrap of pink caught his attention as he circumvented a mound of grass. Coming closer, he realized it was her halter, neatly folded on top of her white shorts. Squinting again, he looked around, then smiled to himself as he saw her. She wasn't washing the plates. She was washing herself.

His desire to vent his anger evaporated as if it had never existed. For a moment, he stood where he was and watched her. She hadn't seen him yet. Alone, she was obviously enjoying herself. She was swimming the way she did everything else—quickly, neatly, with sure, fast strokes. The water parted before her like servants parting before an advancing queen. Her hair was wet and straight, streaming behind her like a dark veil.

She was every man's fantasy.

And his own personal nightmare.

He cupped his hands around his mouth in order for his words to carry to her. "Aren't you afraid that the fish might conduct a reprisal for you killing some of their relatives yesterday?"

Matrice gave a little shriek as she whirled around in the water. The peaceful moment she had been experiencing disintegrated. Though the sky had darkened, the ocean had felt so soothing, that she had completely forgotten about the time. When she'd snuck out of the shack earlier, she had just wanted to wash the sweat from her body. Scott had appeared to be so sound asleep, she was certain she had at least half an hour to herself, if not more.

She eyed her clothes nervously as she tread water. "What are you doing here?"

He grinned, dropping his hands. He could hear her just fine. "Watching you."

She just bet he was, the beast. "Go away."

Rather than do as she asked—or rather, ordered—he thought, Scott sat down next to her clothes. He placed a proprietary hand on the pile. "It's a small island, Crusoe. There aren't that many places for Friday to go."

"Find one."

He shook his head. "Too much trouble."

She was going to make him pay for this. Somehow she was going to make him pay. Big-time. For this and that kiss last night. She glared at him. He wasn't moving. "Go back to the shack."

"In a while."

He was making her nervous, and she wasn't about to give him the satisfaction of getting out while he watched. "I want to get out."

"Go ahead." He waved his hands grandly. "No one's stopping you."

Now he had her really angry. "Scott diMarco, you're no gentleman!"

He leaned back and laughed, enjoying himself for perhaps the first time in months.

"Could be," he agreed readily. "I'm finding out a lot of things about myself that I never knew before, like the fact that I can actually wake up in the morning without the scent of gourmet coffee brewing."

"I don't care!" she shouted. "Just go!"

He pretended not to hear her. "And that I'm beginning to find infuriating women with wild, chestnut hair fascinating."

That took her aback for a minute, until she realized that he was probably laughing at her. "I'm not interested in your likes or dislikes," she snapped. "Scott, I'm getting pruney."

He appeared unmoved. "I thought that was a natural state for a persimmon."

"Scott—"

He heard the pleading note in her voice and took pity on her, though he knew he shouldn't, not after what she had done to him last night. "All right, I'll go." He got to his feet, brushing the coppery grass off his cutoffs. "But I won't like it."

She was beginning to despair that he was never going to leave. "You don't have to like it, just do it!"

The world, he thought as he walked away, resisting the tantalizing temptation to turn around again, lost a terrific field general the day Mary Therese Crusoe became a stockbroker.

Chapter Seven

The sky, Scott noticed as he walked to the shack, was darkening at a rather unnerving rate. Rather than the clear blue that had been there yesterday, shades of deep gray were crossing the brow of the sky like the furrowed forehead of an angry Roman god.

Scott wondered if the storm would break before they got off the island and if the shack could withstand the bout of bad weather if they didn't. He looked at the structure doubtfully as he approached. The edges of the thatched roof were already waving nervously in the rising wind like a woman hurriedly drying her nails.

I hope this wild idea of yours isn't going to kill us, Val.

Walking into the shack, he picked up his T-shirt where it lay crumpled on the ground, and pulled it on. The light coming in through the single window cast a mournful gloom into the shack. He had a bad feeling about this.

Scott looked around the small hut. There wasn't anything he could do about securing it if a storm was coming.

All they could do was stick out the storm and hope for the best.

It seemed insignificantly little to do. He hated this helpless feeling.

Like the feeling, he mused, he had when he was around Matrice. No, there at least he could do something, he told himself. He could resist.

A few minutes later, Matrice entered the shack, blowing in like a hot, tropical storm. Resisting was not as viable an option as he had thought. He looked at the way her clothes were plastered to her body, hugging curves, leaving little to the imagination.

What there was left for the imagination took flight, soaring into fantasies that were best left unexplored. Scott sought refuge in banter. If they were arguing, they couldn't be doing other things.

He touched the tip of her hair. "You look ravishing." She jerked her head back.

Her hair was hanging down about her shoulders and in her eyes. She pushed it out of her face and glared at him. "All right, wise guy, what was all that about back there?" She waved a hand toward the doorway.

He feigned an innocent expression. He enjoyed baiting her. It took his mind off the brewing storm without, and the one that seemed to be brewing just as fiercely within. "All what about?"

He had embarrassed her out there and she wouldn't forgive him for that. Hands fisted at her waist, she leaned forward on her toes like a prizefighter bracing for the bout just ahead. "You were spying on me."

"Since when is swimming considered a covert activity?" He grinned as he thought of the way she'd looked, slicing through the water. "Even in the nude." He saw the way she pressed her lips together in suppressed anger, and he couldn't resist adding, "Peeping, perhaps, but not spying." She looked like Mount Vesuvius, about to erupt. He decided to toss the truth in for good measure. "Besides, I was worried about you."

Yeah, right. So worried that he couldn't peel his eyes away from her while she tread water, waiting for him to leave. "I noticed."

She had no makeup on and was standing in front of him, dripping wet and scowling. Why did he find that so attractive? "No, I mean when I woke up and didn't see you here."

The look on his face was so genuine, she could almost believe that he was telling the truth. But then, that would make her a fool, wouldn't it? She narrowed her eyes, as if that would help her see through to the real reason behind his words. "You were worried?" He nodded. "Why?"

Lightly he rested his arms on her shoulders, bracketing her effectively in between. "I kept asking myself the same thing."

His mouth was so close to hers, she could feel his breath on her lips. She tried to look elsewhere and couldn't. "This is a joke, right?"

Scott took a deep breath. "Depends on what you mean by 'this.' This situation? Yes." Outside, the wind had begun to give voice to its mounting fury. It added to the already growing feeling of isolation. "This feeling pulsating between us? Yes." He could feel it increasing as he said it. "The unsettling way I felt when we kissed last night? Yes."

She felt drugged, hypnotized as she watched his mouth move. "Then what does the 'no' refer to?" she whispered, her pulse scrambling.

He caressed her cheek with the back of his hand. Her skin was like pure silk, he thought. "Our future together."

She had to struggle to keep her eyes from fluttering shut. "I agree."

Nothing outside the shack matched what was happening to him at this moment. It was as if some dark, primal instinct was raging to be set free. "So what do you want to do about it?"

She swallowed, her mouth too dry to form words. "About what?"

His smile was slow, seductive. "The fact that we want to kiss each other again."

She couldn't breathe, couldn't move, but she would go down fighting. "I don't want to kiss you."

He lowered his face to hers, so that their lips almost touched as he spoke. "The hell you don't."

She wet her lips and saw desire flash in his eyes. "I'll prove it to you."

"How?"

"Kiss me and I'll show you just how little I want to kiss you back." If he didn't, if he just backed away and laughed at her, she knew she couldn't be held responsible for her reaction. No court in the world would convict her. At this moment, she wanted him to kiss her more than she wanted anything else in the world.

If he could have been any more aroused, he didn't know how. "Sounds good to me."

But just before his lips covered hers, Matrice placed the flat of her hand on his chest, holding him back. "One thing."

He felt his control shredding. What the hell was happening to him? How could such a little slip of a woman undo him so easily? "What?" he demanded, fighting for patience.

Was it an act? Was this some elaborate charade on his part to snare her and then walk calmly away, washing his hands of her, of the feelings he was creating inside her? The work world she found herself in was full of duplicity. It had taken the edge off her trust. Doubts gnawed at her, even as her body cried out for him. "Why would you want to kiss a woman you find so unappealing?"

That was the trouble. He didn't find her unappealing. She was too damn appealing. But what she also was, was annoying. In spades.

"Penance." He grazed the slope of her throat with his tongue, burning her skin with just the lightest of touches. She tasted salty, like the sea. And he was suddenly hooked on salt forever. "A strong desire for penance." He worked his way to the other side of her throat. He felt, as well as heard, her sigh. "And to atone for whatever sins might be lying around."

"Oh." It was the only word she could manage. Her mind was a complete blank.

Before she could regain any semblance of thought, his lips found hers. And last night's fireworks began all over again.

He hadn't fully realized, even with this ache in his loins, how much he really wanted to simply kiss her again. Until he did it.

It was a little like running out into the path of a hurricane, willingly allowing himself to be sucked up into it. And he was. Completely swept away, though he attempted vainly to keep the upper hand.

There was no upper hand. There was only her, only him and a wealth of emotions in between that were far too complex to untangle.

Damn, he wanted her. And in wanting her, he knew he was forging his own chains, chains that bound him to someone he knew couldn't have cared less. Whatever the consequences, whatever attrition he'd have to make later, he wanted her now.

It was like sitting on a huge palm frond and sliding, pell-mell, down into the mouth of a volcano. The ride took her breath away and the fire that met her burned, consuming her.

Reaching up, she tangled her fingers in his hair, then sighed as his mouth left hers again and pressed a kiss to the throbbing pulse at her throat. She felt as if everything within her was exploding as his tongue lightly glazed the sensitive area. She was losing herself in him and she didn't care. Not now. Later she'd care, when his little cutting words would slice her apart. But for now, she had this. And this was heaven.

It felt as if her blood was roaring in her veins, in her ears.

Dazed, she stopped. This wasn't right. This was too loud. She looked around, trying to focus. It was dark within the shack, but she could still see the quivering walls.

Her breathing still ragged, she turned to Scott. "Is it just me, or is the shack shaking?"

"Both."

His smile faded as he stopped to listen. He heard a keening noise that was growing in volume. It sounded as if it was all around them. The walls trembled before it, like errant servants before a cruel master. He released her and moved from one wall to the next. They were standing, but for how long?

"That's the wind," he murmured needlessly.

He looked out the window. It was as if the sun had completely abandoned the sky and withdrawn to a home obscured by dark, angry clouds. It didn't look good. The tall grass around the shack waved and tangled like an unruly mop of hair. There was an ominous rumbling off in the distance.

Scott turned to look at her. "Offhand, you wouldn't know if this was hurricane season, would you?"

She rubbed her hands up and down her arms, suddenly very cold. "If it's not on the stock exchange, I don't know about it." The feeble joke fell flat. Nervously, she looked around the flimsy shack. They were vulnerable to the elements out here. And there was no other shelter. "Do you think the shack can withstand a storm?"

He seriously doubted it, but then, what did he know? He was used to waiting out storms within structures that had steel girders as underpinnings, not something a beaver would use to build a dam. "That depends on the storm."

That was what she was afraid of. "You're supposed to be reassuring, Friday."

He heard the slight crack in her voice. Could it be that she was afraid? Her? He kept the question to himself and only asked, "You want me to lie?"

"Right now, *yes.*" She said the last word emphatically. She wanted nice, safe words to cling to. She didn't care if they were lies.

Matrice began to pace about the small area, as if that would make the storm retreat. What if there were high waves? A low-lying island could disappear completely.

He saw the fear in her eyes and something within him softened. "Okay," he told her gamely, "the shack can withstand the storm."

She swallowed, unconsciously taking a step closer to him. Somehow it no longer mattered who had the upper hand or got in the last word. It all seemed petty in retrospect. "What do we do?"

The howling seemed relentless. The shack shuddered and shook. "Prayer comes to mind. Beyond that, there's nothing we can do." He had to raise his voice to be heard above the wind. She looked so unsettled, he placed his arm around her shoulders. "Don't worry, it's going to be all right."

She jumped and gasped as a clasp of thunder seemed to roll across the sky right above the shack.

She was terrified, he realized. "You're afraid of thunder." He said the words incredulously. It seemed impossible that a woman who came on so confidently, ready to verbally castrate him, was afraid of something like the peal of thunder. Children were afraid of thunder, not adults.

She wished she could stop trembling. It was noise, only noise. But it seemed to vibrate within every fiber of her being. She tensed as another loud boom echoed around them. Scott held her tighter and she was grateful.

Matrice turned her face toward him, aware of the warmth, the comfort he gave without being asked. "When I was ten, my parents and I went camping. We had one of those rolling trailer homes with all the conveniences. My dad was very big on the outdoors." She knotted her fingers together as she remembered. "Somehow, the second night, I got separated from them. Couldn't find my way back." She spoke haltingly, in short sentences, as if each word was too painful to utter.

"A storm came. I found some shelter. It thundered and rained all night." She pressed her lips together as she felt tears forming. The memory was too vivid, even across the space of over a decade and a half. "My father finally found me at dawn. He'd been out looking all night. I couldn't stop shaking for hours." She tightened her shoulders, as if attempting to withdraw into herself as thunder crashed even closer. She gave Scott a small, deprecating smile. "Thunderstorms remind me of how lost I felt that night. How frightened."

He held her closer, wishing there was something he could do to erase the fear he saw in her eyes. "There's no need to be frightened. I won't leave you."

"You don't have to be this nice," she murmured, embarrassed at being so weak. She smiled her gratitude. "But it helps."

He leaned over and picked up the sleeping bag from the floor. Unzipping it completely, he draped it over both their shoulders. "Let's sit this out," he urged. "It looks like it might last a while."

They sat down on the ground in unison, drawn to one another for warmth, for comfort. She leaned her head against his shoulder. His arm tightened around her as another crack of thunder echoed through the shack. "You can be very nice when you want to be," she said softly.

He stroked her hair. It was beginning to dry and curl around her head. "I was just thinking the same thing about you."

She couldn't let herself get carried away, she thought, even though, for this small interlude, he was being incredibly gentle. And she was so incredibly needy.

The shack shivered, struggling to withstand the force of the angry wind. It was losing the battle. He had to take her mind off this. What did people do when they went camping, anyway? "Know any good camping songs?" he wanted to know.

She shook her head, her eyes never leaving the walls. They were beginning to bend and sway as if dancing to a tempo she couldn't hear. Her mind was a complete blank. "I can't think of any. You?"

"I never went camping."

No, she thought, they had nothing in common. Not when you scratched the surface.

A different sound joined the chorus orchestrated by nature. Rain. It was beginning to rain. Hard. Drops assaulted the shack like pellets fired from a BB gun. They came in through the window and found all the spaces in the roof, christening the interior with a vengeance.

Scott wished that they had a fire going, to take the chill from the air and to bolster Matrice's spirits, but they couldn't build one in the shack. The smoke would only swirl around them, making a bad situation worse, and the rain would eventually put it out, anyway.

The last volley of thunder sounded like cannon fire. Matrice dug her fingers into his T-shirt. "Tell me about your childhood." She needed words to fill the air, to take her mind off what might happen to them if the storm didn't abate. "What did you do when your parents died?"

"Cried."

The word came out without thought, automatically. He had never admitted that to anyone, he realized. He had cried privately, alone in his room, for nights. He'd never even told Valerie, though he knew she'd suspected it at the time. But she had left him his space.

"Valerie and Frank took me in. Frank's my brother." He remembered what it had been like, coming to live with them. He'd been afraid, but Valerie had acted as if he had always belonged there. "They were just married and suddenly they had a twelve-year-old kid to take care of." He smiled fondly, his arms resting lightly along her shoulders. "But Val never complained. She just took me in. Never tried to be my mother, just my friend."

The warmth in his voice had her responding to him. Someone devoid of feelings couldn't talk about a person in those terms. "She sounds wonderful."

He looked at Matrice, pleased with her words. "She is. Except for marooning me out here, she's a pretty terrific lady."

Matrice gasped as the thunder crashed so hard, she could feel it again all over her body. "Easy, easy now," he soothed, talking to her the way he would to a frightened child. Yet there was nothing condescending in his voice. "It's just thunder."

The world went utterly white for a moment, before the darkness returned. "Coupled with just lightning," she added, her breath hitching in her throat. "Oh, God, if it gets any worse, we could be completely submerged in a matter of hours. Hold me, Scott."

"I am holding you," he pointed out gently.

"Tighter."

"Any tighter and I'll be applying a tourniquet." But he did what he could. The edge of the sleeping bag slipped off and he reached over to cover her shoulder again.

Matrice flushed. "You probably think I'm an idiot." She knew she felt like one, but she just couldn't seem to help herself.

His words were kind, understanding. Matrice felt herself unraveling in stages. "Not at this moment, no. Lots of people are afraid of storms."

"They're usually under the age of eight," she said ruefully, wishing the storm would stop. The inside of the shack was growing damper as rain continued coming through the gaps in the roof.

He laughed. When she took these potshots at herself, he could afford to be magnanimous. Besides, right now, she was vulnerable and he wanted to help. "Not all, I'm sure."

She liked the sound of his laughter, the sound of his voice. "What are you afraid of?"

He wanted to say nothing, but this seemed to be a time for truth. It was as if the elements wouldn't brook a lie if he told one. So he didn't. "Growing old by myself."

She looked at him, surprised by the depth of feeling within his voice. It was the last thing she would have expected him to admit to. "You?"

He knew what she was thinking and maybe she had a point. "Contrary to what you might believe, I'm not wrapped up in my work to the exclusion of everything else. I want a home, a family." His eyes drifted to her upturned face. "A wife." His voice lowered as his words made love to her. "Someone with lips that taste of exotic berries. Someone who smells like sin, but has the face of an angel."

Someone like her, he thought.

His hands slowly traveled the length of her throat, until his fingertips just barely cupped her cheek. With his thumb against her chin, he tilted her face up to his and lightly kissed her.

And then it seemed as if the storm was raging within rather than outside the shack.

She forgot about the thunder, forgot about everything except the needs that this man aroused within her with the unnerving speed of a streaking cheetah. Maybe they would die after all, but if they did, she would die in his arms, locked that way for all eternity.

He saw the fire in her eyes. It matched his own.

His hands seemed to burn right through the thin fabric of her halter as he caressed her breasts. She groaned his name, straining against his hand, attempting to absorb his touch, to absorb the comfort that was there for the taking. The rain fell harder and harder, intruding into the swaying shack with more ferocity. The sleeping bag that embraced them both was soaked as their lips found one another. They hardly noticed it.

Above them, the roof creaked and groaned as the wind battered at it with invincible fists, rendering it almost useless. Surrendering against the inevitable, the roof broke apart and flew off. Rain fell on them as if an unseen hand had overturned a bucket filled with water. Without the roof to brace them, the walls collapsed like so many children at the end of ring-around-a-rosy.

He drew the sleeping bag up over their heads. It wasn't much, but it was all they had. Matrice moved closer to him. "Are you all right?" Scott asked.

She nodded, forcing a smile to her lips. He'd been kind when she needed it.

They huddled together, two against the elements, waiting for the inevitable to happen, facing it bravely because they were together. Somehow that helped. And then, just as abruptly as the storm had started, it stopped. The wind died down as the rain began to subside. The storm had blown itself out to sea.

She looked at him and began to laugh, her tension flowing out of her like water through an opening in a dam.

Her laugh was infectious and he joined her. "What's so funny?"

"You look like a drowned rat."

He shook his head as he continued laughing. Leaning forward, he pushed the plastered hair away from her face. "I wouldn't throw rocks if I were you." Cupping her face in his hands, he grinned. "I think we're going to make it after all, Ms. Crusoe." He lowered his mouth to hers, brushing a kiss against her lips. "We've got a lot of work on our hands."

She felt like laughing and crying at the same time. The storm was over and they were all right. "Meaning?"

"The shack." He gestured around. "We're going to have to rebuild it somehow. There's no telling how long we're going to be here before we're finally 'rescued.'"

She nodded. We. He said it so easily. She supposed that, while they were on the island, there was no harm in—

Scott held his hand up. He thought he heard something. He turned his head and concentrated. "Listen."

She looked up at the sky, afraid the storm was returning. "What?"

He dropped his hands and rose. "Do you hear a motor?" he asked as he extended a hand to her.

She took the hand he offered and got up. She heard nothing. "I've been hearing the sound of a motor for twenty-four hours now. It's called wishful thinking."

He strained to hear it and was rewarded. That was definitely the sound of a motor. "No, it's called an outboard motor."

She opened her mouth to protest, then stopped. He was right. She *could* hear something, a noise that was getting louder. She was afraid to hope. "Do you think they've come back for us?"

He was already striding past where the shack's threshold had been only minutes before. "If they haven't, I'm invoking justifiable homicide when they do."

Matrice quickly fell into step beside him. "Get in line."

The rain, so relentless and cruel before, now fell in the light, steady tempo ascribed to the gentle summer rains. As they walked toward the sound of the motorboat, they found pieces of the shack scattered about like so many parts of a broken toy.

Matrice grabbed Scott's arm, her fingers digging into his flesh as she made out a shape on the ocean. "It's a boat, Friday. A big cruiser."

He shaded his eyes against the rain and looked at the ocean. "It doesn't look like Val's boat."

"That's because it's the Coast Guard." Her mother was far too inexperienced to pilot a boat through choppy waters. They had obviously called for help.

Scott and Matrice ran the rest of the way to the shore. Mixed emotions churned through Matrice and she didn't even bother attempting to sort them out. All except those dealing with her mother. When the woman came running toward her—along with someone who had to be Scott's sister-in-law—she didn't know whether to hug her for finally arriving with help, or strangle her for putting her in this island to begin with.

One look at her mother's frantic expression settled the matter for her.

Rita Crusoe threw her arms around her only child, silently offering up a prayer of thanksgiving as she hugged her. "Oh, God, Mary Therese, I thought you were dead." Rita had lived through a thousand nightmares in the space of a few hours, ever since she'd heard the morning weather forecast.

Valerie hugged Scott hard. Relief shimmered like a precious pearl within an oyster. She'd been so afraid that her innocent plotting had cost her the life of someone she loved dearly. She stood back, scanning his face and body as if taking inventory of everything. "Scottie, are you all right?" She bit back a sob.

A fortyish man in a white Coast Guard uniform stood behind the two women. "Are either of you hurt?"

"We're fine," Scott assured them all. Now that it was over with, he could make light of the situation. Or at least, he amended, glancing briefly at Matrice, part of the situation. He jerked his thumb over his shoulder. "But the shack died."

Rita didn't care about the shack. Just as long as they were both alive and well. Rita blinked tears from her eyes. They mingled with the rain. "We called the Coast Guard as soon as we heard the weather report."

"When we planned this, the bureau said there was supposed to be fair weather this weekend. This storm was supposed to hit later in the week and much farther down south," Valerie put in, taking hold of each of them by the arm as they all began to walk toward the boat.

It might not have been a hurricane, but it was as close as he'd care to come to one, given the circumstances. "Obviously the storm hadn't read the weather report."

Rita stopped at the foot of the dock. Part of it had been torn away by the storm, fodder for an angry giant breaking whatever came in its way. "But you *are* all right?" Rita asked again. She looked from one to the other, assuring herself that they were and searching for signs of other things.

Matrice and Scott exchanged glances. With the danger over, an awkwardness was setting in quickly, pushing away the intimacy, the interdependency they had shared so briefly. They had said things to each other in the heat of the moment, exposed themselves far more than either one was ready to because of the situation. Now those things hung between them, barriers sending them back to their corners.

Matrice turned away first. "Yes, just get us off this god-forsaken piece of land." Shivering, she accepted the coast-guard's hand and climbed into the boat. She was escorted into the boat's cabin. Rita followed.

"Scott?" Valerie turned to him, concerned. She searched his face, wondering what had happened here besides a summer storm.

He set his mouth hard. It was time to get back to civilization. To his life. He gestured his sister-in-law toward the boat. "You heard the lady. Let's get out of here."

Val placed her hand on his arm, unmindful of the rain. She'd been wet before. But there was something in Scott's eyes that troubled her. "Are you all right?"

He knew she wasn't asking about his physical state. "I'll let you know when I find out."

She knew the matter was closed for now. Valerie said nothing further as she got on board ahead of him. The captain turned the boat around, heading for the mainland.

Within the cabin, the captain provided blankets for Matrice and Scott and dispensed coffee. Valerie chattered brightly. Her tone didn't fool Scott, but he said nothing. Taking his coffee, he sat down on the bench. Matrice sat, huddled and nursing her own cup, on the opposite end.

Valerie frowned as she studied their body language. She and Rita had failed, she thought. She had no interest in the cup of coffee the young guardsman handed her.

Rita took Matrice's hand. "We're so sorry." A mother's anguish was in her voice. "If anything would have happened to either one of you, we couldn't have lived with ourselves."

Matrice sat, letting the steam rising from the coffee cup warm her face. Nothing was going to warm her heart, but that was life. Her mother's words echoed in her mind. Something *had* happened out there. Something she didn't want to talk about or even think about until she had had a warm shower and dry clothes.

And maybe not even then.

She was closing up, he could see it, Scott thought, glancing at Matrice as he lifted the cup to his lips. The interlude on the island had been nothing more than that, just an interlude. She would go back to being herself, a waspish overbearing woman who thought she knew it all. He could tell by the way she was avoiding his eyes. She would go back to her belittling remarks, to dismissing him. Well, who needed her?

He took a deep drink from his cup. "Fortunately, nothing did happen."

Nothing. He called tearing up her soul nothing. Kissing her until she was senseless, nothing. If the storm hadn't hit just then and the shack exploded around them, they would have wound up making love this morning. And he called that nothing.

She'd been right. He was just testing her, seeing how far she would go. Lying to her. He was probably going to laugh about this, and her, over lunch with his buddies at work tomorrow.

Matrice shivered and pulled the blanket tighter around her, trying not to remember how his arms had felt in its place. "That's right," she said dully. "Nothing happened."

Chapter Eight

Life wasn't getting back to normal.

Oh, the frantic rush was there, the hectic pace that had been a part of his life since he'd begun working on Wall Street. But that wasn't Scott's problem. The problem was in his head.

It had been an entire week since he had left the island and Matrice behind. The week had been filled with minicrises on the market, a client who needed to be soothed and so much work that it felt as if the telephone had become a permanent part of his anatomy. Enough work to drown in. Enough work, certainly, to wipe out every extraneous thought that might want to struggle to the fore and haunt him.

Yet he couldn't stop thinking about her. He might as well be stranded on the island.

It wasn't just that her image snuck up on him at odd, unguarded moments, intruding on his thoughts. She *was* his thoughts. All of them. Over and over, like a never-ending summer rerun, he kept reliving the short time they had spent together on the island. Every glimmer, every gesture, every nuance was magnified, like a faraway scene brought close by high-power binoculars.

He pushed aside a stack of color-coded folders on his desk. Two of them tumbled off, the correspondence within fanning out as they fell on the floor. He didn't bother to pick them up. Instead, he buried his face in his hands. He was going to go crazy and he hadn't the slightest idea what to do about it.

Getting in touch with her was out of the question. She hadn't even bothered to say goodbye when they'd docked. She had walked off without so much as a backward glance. Hell would need a new heating system before he picked up the phone to call her.

He felt he was already there.

Scott realized that someone was knocking on his door and had been knocking for the last couple of minutes. He raised his head and saw Jerry Meyers standing in the doorway, looking at him quizzically through his wire-rimmed glasses.

Jerry leaned into the room. "You okay?"

"Just a little stressed out, that's all. T.G.I.F." Scott quirked his lips into a halfhearted smile. So it was Friday, so what? That left him the entire weekend to sit around and think. He didn't want to do that. Maybe he'd get together with Val, Frank and the kids and take them all out for a day at the ballpark or something. The idea lifted his spirits marginally.

Jerry walked into the small office and saw the folders scattered on the floor. "Redecorating?" He looked at Scott's face. The man looked worn from the inside out. "God, you really do look like you need a break. Pat Sullivan's giving a big blowout tonight. D'you want to come?"

Scott shook his head. With a sigh, he bent and picked up the folders, then tossed them onto his desk. He'd sort out the letters later. "No, I think I'll pass." He was not in a very sociable mood.

Planting himself on the corner of Scott's desk, Jerry gave the appearance of a man who was not going to take no for an answer. He looked at his friend with concern. There'd been too many good people who'd burned out in this line of work. He didn't want to see Scott become another disability statistic.

"C'mon, it'll do you good," he urged. "Nothing formal. Just a bunch of people getting together. A lot of noise, a lot of food, maybe even some good conversation in between innings."

Scott looked up. The last word had caught his interest. "Innings?"

Jerry grinned like a deep-sea fisherman who finally felt a strong tug on his line after hours of angling. "Did I forget to mention that Sullivan's renting a big-screen TV so that we can all watch the play-offs?"

"You did." Scott leaned back in his chair, then glanced at his desk calendar. He didn't even know what season it was anymore. "Is it that time of year already?"

Jerry shook his head and laughed. "Man, you do need some time off."

No, he didn't, Scott thought. Time off would give him more time to think and he was tired of thinking, tired of wrestling with emotions that were totally out of place. He didn't need time; he needed order and something to keep his mind occupied until it was restored. Maybe a party was just the thing he did need.

He grinned as he laced his fingers behind his neck and rocked in the chair. "Talked me into it, Jerry. Sullivan's moved, hasn't he?" Jerry nodded. "Where is it and what time should I be there?"

Jerry scribbled the address boldly across Scott's note-pad. "Here, don't lose this." He pushed the entire pad to-ward him. "Game starts at six-thirty. Anytime around then should be all right." Jerry turned toward the doorway, then stopped and looked at Scott. "See you there?"

"You bet." Scott nodded as he folded the paper and placed it in his wallet.

The address Jerry gave him belonged to an apartment building located in one of the more exclusive parts of the city. Also possibly one of the deafer parts of the city, Scott thought as he rang the bell again. This time, he leaned on it for the count of five. A cacophony of voices was ema-nating from the apartment. The door almost vibrated with the noise. It reminded him of the way the shack had shud-dered during the storm.

Maybe this wasn't such a good idea.

Scott was about to give up when the door suddenly opened. The young, sexy blonde who opened the door looked instantly intrigued. Her wide, blue eyes slid up and down his body with practiced speed as her red-lacquered lips parted in an inviting smile. "Hi."

He wasn't certain if she said the word or simply exhaled it. "Hi." He wondered if he had the right address. The last time he had gotten together with Sullivan, the man had lived over a delicatessen. Three years and a lucrative ca-reer had changed all that. "Jerry Meyers said that there was a play-off party here."

"There is if you want there to be." She laughed at her own words and tossed her head so that her long hair would drape over her shoulder. Huge dangling earrings threat-ened to inflict wounds on his arm as they sliced the air near him before settling into place.

The woman wrapped both her arms around his and drew him into the room as she pushed the door closed behind her. "I'm Terry." She cocked her head, waiting for him to respond with his name.

"Scott." He watched in fascination as she righted her head again. It seemed like an extraordinary feat, given the weight of her earrings. She wore four in each ear. Three small hoops and something that might have served as a chandelier in a midsize restaurant. She was looking at him as if he were the special of the day.

Scott looked around, trying to sort out faces. The foyer and living room beyond were crammed full of bodies. "Is Jerry here yet?"

She lifted her shoulders carelessly and let them drop again. Her thin, rib-fitting white blouse slide off one shoulder. She left it there. "I wouldn't know. Why don't we mingle and find out?" Her arms still encircling his, she pressed her breasts against him and smiled.

The woman wasn't wearing a bra. Scott silently declined the blatant invitation. "I'm meeting someone else here, as well."

Terry cocked her head again. Her left earring slid along her bare shoulder. "Female?"

He thought of the way Matrice had looked swimming in the ocean, water glistening on her nude body like tiny crystals. "Definitely."

"Oh." Terry didn't bother to hide her regret as she released her hold on his arm. "Well—" she shrugged philosophically "—look me up if she doesn't show."

She gave a short tug on an even shorter spandex skirt and meandered off, her hips swaying seductively to the strains of the national anthem. The game on the screen was just beginning.

What was the matter with him? Scott thought. He had just turned his back on what could have been a very entertaining, very meaningless few hours, no strings attached. The lady looked as if all she wanted was a good time and nothing beyond that. It would have been just what he needed to get his mind off Matrice.

But he wasn't like that, not anymore. His mind had turned down a more serious avenue.

His mind was also illogical and beyond hope, he was beginning to think as he slowly maneuvered his way into the living room, tortured the way it was by images of Matrice.

Why it should even *be* on Matrice was beyond his understanding. He had spent only about thirty-six hours with the woman. Granted, it had been a very intense thirty-six hours, but he had spent more time, collectively, sitting in his dentist's chair than he had in her company and he certainly didn't have images of his dentist preying on his mind every waking minute.

Every sleeping minute, too, he thought with a note of annoyed despair.

Passing a side table, Scott picked up a handful of pretzels and nibbled as he nodded at several people he knew. As he scanned the immediate area, really focusing for the first time, he realized that there were actually quite a few people he knew here.

Yet he felt alone.

As alone as a man on a completely deserted island. Just what the hell had happened to him during that short time to keep him from functioning the way he had before he'd allowed Valerie to maroon him with that harpy?

He heard a low, throaty laugh and the noise within the room suddenly seemed to fade into the background. He looked toward the direction it had come from, his pulse quickening just the slightest bit as he damned himself for it. Now he was even imagining that she was here.

She *was* here.

Like a kamikaze fighter pilot with but a single mission, Scott began nudging people aside as he made his way over to the far corner of the living room. To his destiny. To his undoing. To Matrice.

She had seen him. The moment Scott had entered the apartment with that blonde draped all over him, she had seen him. She frowned. It certainly didn't look as if it had taken him long to get back into the swing of things again. And it hurt.

She sucked the remnants of a diet soda through her straw, filtering the few drops over the pile of ice chips. Not like her, she thought. She hadn't been able to get into the swing of anything since she'd returned. He had entirely messed up her mind.

Even with the new country emerging from the crumbling shambles of the old world power and the stock market zig-zagging in response, all Matrice could think of was the overgrown oaf. The way he had held her in his arms during the storm. The way he had kissed her with an ardor that practically dissolved her teeth. She had spent seven days thinking of nothing else but him and he was waltzing around with bimbos in see-through blouses and microminis or whatever that thing was that she was barely wearing.

Matrice let out a sigh. She should have never listened to Moira and come to this party. She didn't belong here even though she loved baseball and half the people here were friends, or at least acquaintances. Like Rip Van Winkle who had slept past his time, she didn't seem to belong anywhere anymore.

It was time to go home. She set down her glass and started for the door. As she turned, she felt a hand on her arm. She didn't have to look to know who it was. The memory of his touch was indelibly burned into her heart. She refused to turn around.

If he hadn't caught her, he was certain she would have slipped away again and he couldn't let her do that. Though he had sworn to himself never to have anything to do with her again, now that he had seen her, he couldn't let her just go. "Matrice, wait."

She forced herself to smile before she turned around. She'd be damned if she let him see what he was doing to her. He didn't deserve that kind of victory, especially not at her expense.

"Oh, hello." She greeted him in the same sort of tone she might have used with the mailman, perhaps even a shade more distant. "I was just leaving."

Tongue-tied, he was at a loss for a second. She was wearing a navy blue top over jeans just tight enough to remind him of the way she had looked the morning he'd happened upon her in the ocean. "I was just coming in—"

"Yes, I saw."

They were waltzing around words like two strangers instead of two people who had shared a life-threatening situation. He saw her begin to edge away toward the door and kept his hand on her arm. "Well, you look none the worse for our ordeal."

A hell of a lot you know. The man was myopic, she decided. Or he just didn't care. "Neither do you," she answered brightly, her smile tight. "As a matter of fact, you seem to have bounced back rather well."

He knew that tone. She was trying to tell him something, but for the life of him, he had no idea what. This time, he asked. "What do you mean by that?"

Did he like rubbing her face in it? she wondered. Of course he did. Why else would he ask?

"Aren't you afraid your girlfriend will get cold?" She pretended to look around for the woman. In this crowd, she'd be difficult to find. "She seemed to be almost percolating when you walked in."

Matrice was making as little sense now as she had at their first meeting. "Girlfriend?"

"The girl without a spine. The one who was poured all over you as you walked in just now." She attempted to keep a disinterested tone in her voice. How could he lower himself to go out with someone like that when he had kissed her with such bone-melting passion on the island just a week ago? Her hurt felt raw and palpitating as she added, "I'm really surprised your taste runs so shallow, but then, I suppose like attracts like."

He was about to disclaim all knowledge of the woman she was referring to, but Matrice's words put him on edge. So what else was new? It was just as he'd suspected. The two of them couldn't be together in a room with real walls without being at each other's throats.

Perverseness had him saying, "She happens to have a doctorate in philosophy."

Matrice frowned. If he thought she believed that, the next thing he would do was attempt to sell her junk bonds. "She looks very deep," she said sarcastically. What did she care who or what he was going out with? The man meant nothing to her. Nothing. "Well, I have to go."

She said it in such a bored voice, he wanted to strangle her. "I suppose you have a hot date waiting."

Her eyes narrowed. The way he said it told her that Scott didn't believe she had a date at all. "Two. One for each arm. I don't believe in wasting any time." She turned on her heel, damning him as she pushed past a man in her path.

Scott watched her go. He was well rid of her. That was the reason he had come in the first place, to forget he had ever met her. And here she was, taunting him. He was better off with her leaving. Now maybe he could relax.

With an angry huff, he followed her, telling himself that he needed to be committed for exhibiting clearly masochistic tendencies. "Matrice, wait," he called after her.

She stopped, knowing she shouldn't. Where was her common sense when she needed it? "Why?"

He didn't know why. He just knew he wanted her to stay. When she wouldn't turn to face him, he maneuvered around so that he could face her. He thought he saw the slightest glimmer of hurt in her eyes before she managed to erase it. Hurt? Her? A microscopic bit of hope began to form.

"I don't know that woman. She just opened the door for me when I rang the bell. I don't know if she's a philosophy major or a ditch digger."

Matrice fervently hoped that his relieved feeling she was experiencing didn't show. "Neither probably." She looked toward the door and hesitated.

"Are you still leaving?"

She really hadn't wanted to leave, not if she was being honest with herself. She had no one to go home to but the dog. "Maybe I can stay for a few more minutes."

He picked up a can of beer from a cooler with one hand and a diet soda with the other, then offered Matrice her choice. She took the soda. He popped the top on the beer. "What about your two dates?" He grinned as he asked.

She knew he had seen through the ruse even as she uttered the words. "They can go out with each other."

He motioned her back into the living room. They forged their way past several groups huddled by the snack bar until they came to one of the sofas. Scott perched on the arm, letting her have the only seat. Behind them, the television announcer reeled off vital statistics as the two teams prepared to square off. "So, what've you been doing since our rescue?"

She held the can between her hands, rubbing it back and forth. The awkwardness that had seeped in after the storm had abated on the island was still there. She'd shown him how vulnerable she was. Worse, she'd let him know how easily he could have had her. "Same thing you have."

He doubted it. She didn't look as if she had spent seven near sleepless nights, haunted by a warm, giving mouth attached to a woman who wouldn't give an inch.

His throat was dry. He nodded, taking a sip of beer. When in doubt, talk shop, he thought. "I know what you mean. The stock market's been going nuts all week. I don't understand it." Because he hadn't attempted to sort it out, he added silently. His head hadn't been clear enough for that.

Here, at least, she had some confidence. "It's very simple, really," she began and saw a frown forming on his lips. Now what was his problem? Didn't he like taking advice from a woman? Was he like all the other men she worked with, constantly needing to be shown that she was as "up" in this field, if not more so, as they?

She was being condescending again. Why did he keep hoping that things would be different? No matter what was said, they always came back to this attitude problem she had when it came to him.

"That was just a figure of speech," he began testily.

The crack of the bat behind him had Matrice looking around his shoulder at the screen. He glanced in that direction, then at her. She had suddenly come to life, energized, as she followed the action on the screen.

"C'mon, Wayne, you can make it," she cried, cheering a runner around the bases as he made for home plate.

Maybe Val had done a little research at that. Baseball, when he had had the time, had been his major passion. "I take it you like baseball?"

She grinned as the player slid across the plate, foiling the catcher's attempt to tag him out. Matrice let out a triumphant breath, having run the bases vicariously. "Love it."

Scott hadn't paid attention to which side was up. He nodded toward the screen. "Rooting for the Mets?"

She looked at him incredulously. Obviously he related to underdogs, or thought she did. "Are you crazy? They haven't a prayer. The Giants'll cream them."

He shook his head, for once seeing the humor in the situation. Even when they found an area they agreed on, they disagreed. It seemed par for the course. Scott made himself as comfortable as possible and started to watch the game.

When the woman sitting next to Matrice rose, Scott opened his mouth to tell her to scoot over. Before he could say anything, the seat was taken by a tall, impeccably dressed man whose casual clothing bespoke of high-priced designer labels. Holding a glass of beer in one hand rather than a can, he looked as if he had just stepped out of a department store window.

"Matrice, where have you been hiding yourself?" The man leaned over to kiss her.

Scott's hand tightened on his beer can, denting it in the middle.

Matrice moved her head at the last moment so that the man's lips brushed against her hair instead of her cheek. "Hello, Wyatt."

Scott noted the pained expression on Matrice's face and wondered if she was uncomfortable because he was here to witness this, or because the other man was here. He decided to wait for a few minutes to watch rather than dump his can of beer on the pompous idiot.

Matrice looked up at Scott, wishing he could say something to make the other man go away. No such luck. Stuck, she introduced them. "Wyatt Houghton, Scott diMarco."

Playing along, Scott smiled broadly as he leaned over to shake the other man's hand.

"Co-workers?" Wyatt asked Matrice, barely touching his hand to Scott's.

The man had soft, fleshy hands, Scott thought, stifling an urge to wipe his against his jeans. "Arch-rivals, actually." Scott grinned at Matrice. "We're having a showdown at the O.K. Corral tonight at midnight."

Wyatt spared Scott a bored look. "Droll." He turned his attention to Matrice, completely shutting Scott out as he snaked his arm around her shoulders. "So, don't you ever listen to your answering machine? I've been trying to reach you for weeks."

Matrice leaned forward. The man made her skin feel as if it could crawl away under its own power just to escape him. "I've been exceedingly busy."

She threw Scott a silent plea for help. Scott gave her an amused look in response and took another sip of beer to quell what felt like the beginnings of jealousy.

"Not too busy to party I see," Wyatt pointed out, pouting. And then the slight protrusion of his lower lip vanished as he drew closer to her. "Maybe we could get away a little later and take up where I left off."

Obviously, Scott intended to watch her suffer through this. Why had she thought otherwise?

As Wyatt began crowding her on the sofa, Matrice got to her feet, vividly recalling their one and only date. "You didn't leave off, Wyatt, you were pushed off."

He ran his palm along his smoothed blond hair, curbing an annoyed expression as his eyes darted toward Scott. "You wound me."

She took a step back and bumped into a table. Potato chips rained down behind her on the rug. "No, but I wanted to."

Wyatt was on his feet, grabbing her hand insistently. "Come one, Matrice, I won't take no for an answer this time." The expression on his perfectly chiseled face was between a smirk and a leer. Scott wanted to erase both of them with his fist. "You don't know what you're missing."

Enough of sitting on the sideline. He'd never entertained a violent thought in his life but stringing this man up by his armpits suddenly had great appeal. "The lady said no, *Wyatt.*"

Wyatt gave him a belittling look. "I don't see how this is any of your business, Marcus."

Scott placed himself between Matrice and Wyatt. "It's diMarco," he corrected, his voice low and threatening, "and she's my fiancée. That makes it my business."

Matrice's head snapped in Scott's direction, her eyes opened wide in astonishment.

Wyatt's brown eyes narrowed beneath perfectly shaped eyebrows whose maintenance was part of his morning ritual. He looked at Matrice. "Is this true?"

Any port in a storm, Matrice thought, even a preposterous one. She was quick to position herself next to Scott. Scott placed his arm around her shoulders and drew her closer. She tried not to think about how much she'd missed that. "Absolutely."

Wyatt looked unconvinced. "When's the wedding?"

Leery of citing a date that would contradict Scott's answer if he responded at the same time as she, Matrice said, "We'll send you an invitation."

"Be sure that you do." Wyatt attempted to regain face. "Congratulations," he said coldly. "But I'd keep my number handy if I were you, Matrice."

"Absolutely," she promised. "I never know when I might need some kindling."

Wyatt turned and left in a huff.

Scott didn't move his arm. It felt as if it belonged there. "Nicely done."

She had to concentrate not to let herself drift off. It felt so good to have him so near to her like this, but it was just for a ruse, she reminded herself.

"I could say the same," she told him. Out of the corner of her eye she saw Wyatt talking to someone and gesturing in their direction. An uneasy feeling began to take hold, but she shook it off. She turned her face up to Scott's. "But what made you say something like that?"

He wanted to kiss her here and now, but refrained. She'd probably only say something to mock him if he did. "It was the most outlandish thing I could think of."

Was it so farfetched? Did she repel him that much? "Right."

He hated the fact that she agreed so readily. "Besides, I don't think he would have backed off if I had called you my girl."

She shook her head. His girl. It had an odd appeal, but she knew he was only making fun of the situation. "Too old-fashioned."

He found himself reacting to the way she blatantly dismissed being coupled with him. He retaliated. "Too unbelievable," he corrected.

She squared her shoulders. "But being your fiancée isn't?"

He had lost his way in this argument, he thought, as well as all reason. "I didn't say I was logical. It was a split-second save, remember?"

She knew she should be grateful. It was just that he made her so angry. "Sorry, you did do me a big favor." She shivered as she remembered her evening with Wyatt, what there had been of it before she cut him dead. "The man gives octopi a bad name."

Scott just couldn't see her with the man. The fact that she had been with him bothered Scott more than he wanted to admit, even to himself. "Doesn't say much for your taste in men."

She bit off another retort. She owed him one and would be gracious even if it killed her. Or until she killed him. Then she noticed that his can was dented in the middle, as if he had grasped it too hard and she smiled to herself. "A friend set me up. The key phrase, you will note, is 'set me up.'"

So, she hadn't gone out with that character by her own choice. The information pleased him and he relaxed a little. "Didn't she like you?"

Matrice laughed. "I'm beginning to have my doubts. Now, where were we before you so gallantly rode to my rescue?"

He grinned. "I figured it was part of my duties as your man Friday," he said, reminding her of the term she'd bestowed on him on the island—the one he'd balked at the time. "I believe we were arguing."

"I know that. We're always arguing." She said the words fondly and, in an odd way, there was almost a comforting feeling about that, though if someone asked, she couldn't say why. "But about what?"

Scott looked into her eyes. He didn't want to argue. He had better things on his mind to do with her. "Beats me."

Someone booed a play at third and she remembered. "Oh, the Mets." She gave him a superior look. "That's right. You think they're going to win."

"Remember '69?"

"How could I remember? I was only four."

"It's a rhetorical question."

"It's a dumb question if you think that history'll repeat itself." She was beginning to enjoy this, she thought.

Scott twirled an imaginary moustache. "Care to make a little wager?"

"You mean put my money where my mouth is?" She stopped. The last time she had said those words to him, he had kissed her. From the look on his face, he remembered, too.

Scott turned so that he was facing her, their bodies touching. "Now you're finally making some sense."

Electricity that would have made the island storm's pale by comparison hummed between them as he lowered his mouth to hers. The sound akin to a gong being hit jarred him to a halt.

"Hey, everybody!"

Scott turned to see their host, Patrick Sullivan, standing in the middle of the room. He had what appeared to be a small dinner gong in his hand and hit it again to make sure he had everyone's attention.

"I have an announcement to make." The sturdily built man looked around, pausing dramatically. "Guess who's getting married?"

A surge of voices tripped over one another as they shouted out different names, but Pat shook his head, looking very smug and pleased with himself to be the bearer of the news.

"Nope, none of the above. It's your favorite stockbroker and mine, Scott diMarco." Scanning, he located Scott in the room and pointed him out. "Scratch him off your list ladies, he belongs to Patrice Crusoe now."

"That's Matrice," Matrice called out, automatically correcting Pat before she realized the significance of her correction. She was verifying his announcement.

Matrice and Scott looked at one another in unspoken horror and distress.

Chapter Nine

Matrice moved closer to Scott. "Now what?" she murmured. It felt as if the entire room was converging around them to offer their congratulations.

His hand was being swallowed up by grasping hands and shaken like the handle of an old-fashioned pump that was frantically being primed for water. "We collect wedding gifts?" he suggested to her in a stage whisper.

He was obviously enjoying this predicament, she thought. Why didn't that surprise her? A pasted smile on her face, she thanked each well-wisher, mumbling something unintelligible in response, wishing she could get away.

"God, Scott, I never thought you'd actually ever do it."

"Got yourself one classy-looking lady, there, pal."

"Why didn't you tell me?" The last question came from Jerry as he pushed his way forward through the crowd.

"We weren't sure until just now," Scott answered without missing a beat.

The man lied much too well to ever be trusted, Matrice thought. "You're not taking this seriously," she hissed, averting her face so that only he could hear her.

He hadn't seen her lips move at all. It was a trick she had probably learned early as a child. That way her lips didn't get tired when she rambled on, nonstop, he mused. "I'm desperately trying not to," he answered in the same hushed tones.

"Congratulations, Matrice. He's a hunk." Moira declared.

Matrice raised her eyes to Scott and saw that despite the general cacophony of noise, he had singled out the compliment.

"He'll do," she answered.

Scott bent down. "Maybe you'd like me to call Wyatt back and tell him this was all a hoax for his benefit," he whispered into her ear.

"No!"

Several people looked startled by her loud declaration. Scott grinned. "I was just telling her I might have to postpone the wedding date."

She felt an uncontrollable urge to beat on him. Given the amount of witnesses, she refrained.

The congratulations went on for almost half an inning. When the side retired, so did Scott and Matrice. He took her by the elbow and ushered her toward the sofa again. Their spot had been taken by Jerry and the blonde who had greeted him at the door.

"Why don't you two find a closet and neck?" Jerry's grin was so wide, the sprinkling of red freckles on his face were stretched thin. "I've yet to get to know my perfect mate."

"That makes two of us, Jerry," Scott said under his breath as he and Matrice moved away.

"And what's that supposed to mean?" She took offense at his tone, although his words were simple enough to understand.

"Just that we don't know each other very well, my sweet."

And it would undoubtedly stay that way, she thought. Well, at least he hadn't humiliated her by announcing to the group that it was all a horrible mistake. And while it *was* a horrible mistake that seemed to be swelling on them like a hot-air balloon preparing for flight, she couldn't help wondering why he hadn't tried to rectify it immediately. After all, it had been his lie.

Uttered to save her from Wyatt, she ruefully remembered. He had ridden to her rescue just as he had on the island during the storm, when she needed him most. And was being flippant about it. She just couldn't figure him out.

"Don't forget to invite me to the wedding!" someone called out to them from across the room.

It had to be one of Scott's friends, Matrice thought, because she didn't recognize the man. She felt her arm being taken as Scott directed her away from another couple heading their way who seemed about to engage them in conversation.

They found sanctuary in the kitchen.

"Well, this is another fine mess you've gotten me into." He laughed as he dumped the remainder of his beer into the sink. He was more amused, than anything else, at the turn of events.

She didn't see anything funny about the situation. "This is no time to play Laurel and Hardy."

He pulled a paper towel from the roll and wiped his hands. "You watch Laurel and Hardy?" It didn't seem like the kind of entertainment she would enjoy. He could envision her enjoying some avant-garde comedy program that made no sense to him.

"Watched," she corrected. "When I had a life." Which she didn't seem to any more, not with work crowding every moment that wasn't filled with thoughts of him. She sat down on one of the two free chairs surrounding the table. The others were covered with newspapers and magazines, apparently hastily deposited there from the table in order to make room for the extra trays of food. "Besides, don't change the subject."

"All right." He straddled the other chair and faced her. "On the subject then, you got me into this, not the other way around.

"How?" She hadn't been the one to lie, he had. Matrice eyed a corned beef sandwich and thought better of it. The knot in her stomach wouldn't let her consume anything at the moment.

He rested his arms across the back of the chair, studying her. No, his assessment of her on the island hadn't been wrong. She was beautiful. But that wasn't going to sway him. Male spiders were probably attracted in the same manner to mate with black widows, but he had no intention of becoming a casualty because of his own natural urges. "I had to save you from that giant blowfish Wyatt, didn't I?"

Why had he? Did he want to hold something over her? She couldn't fathom another reason, not one that made sense to her. "What's done is done, I suppose. But what do we do now?"

He shrugged. The whole thing seemed to bother her a great deal more than it did him. Which meant she probably didn't want to be associated with him. Probably thought herself too good for him. He cut himself a quarter of a heaping sandwich and took a bite. A tiny glob of mustard squirted out on his fingers.

"Stay engaged for a reasonable amount of time, have a huge argument and call off the wedding." He finished the piece in three bites. "Everyone saves face."

She watched, hypnotized, as he licked the dab of mustard from his fingers, and felt herself getting aroused. She reached for a napkin and handed it to Scott, wishing herself immune to him. "I don't think the argument part is going to be difficult. It's the staying engaged for a reasonable amount of time that will be."

He had seen desire flicker in her eyes and grinned. She might act as if she considered him an irritant, but she was obviously reacting to him on another level and that pleased him. He didn't want to be alone in his misery. "Everyone has their own definition of reasonable." Something goaded him into adding, "You're not mine."

No, the arguing part was not going to be a problem at all. "The feeling is mutual."

He wadded the napkin and tossed it toward the garbage. The blue paper ball landed on the overflowing pile, then fell off. "Ah, another thing we have in common." He rose and retrieved the napkin, then placed it on top again. He hooked his thumbs on his pockets and looked at Matrice. "Want to watch the rest of the game?"

She looked over her shoulder at the darkened living room, filled with people who thought she was engaged. "Not anymore."

He nodded. "All right, I'll take you home."

She hadn't expected him to make the offer. "I came with a girlfriend."

He took her arm. "How would it look if I let my fiancée go home with her friend?"

"Like I suddenly came to my senses." She relented. If she was involved in this charade, at least for a couple of days, she might as well play along. "I suppose you're right."

It took her a long time to come around, he thought with a grin. "First sensible thing you've said all night. Perhaps even in your lifetime."

He was back in form again, she thought. It hadn't taken long. She looked around the living room for Moira to tell her she was leaving. She saw the redhead in the corner, talking to another couple and waved to get her attention. "The most sensible thing I could have said was no to my mother right from the start."

Scott shook his head philosophically. "Too late now for both of us."

Matrice stopped and looked at the strangely serious expression on his face. Why did she feel as if that was somehow prophetic?

Matrice unlocked her door and then paused. "Would you like to come in?"

She voiced the invitation automatically, then thought better of it. Well, it was too late now, she thought. Maybe she was trying to prove to herself that what she'd experienced on the island had only been some sort of fleeting reaction to being marooned with a good-looking man—nothing more. Now that there were choices, he certainly wouldn't be hers.

"Sure, why not?" He walked in behind her. "I've never—"

He stopped as his leg was accosted by a small furry animal. The dog wasn't trying to bite him, Scott realized, it was attempting to climb him. Paws outstretched to reach just a little past Scott's kneecap, the dog's tail thumped madly on the hardwood floor like a metronome gone amok. "I take it this is your watchdog?"

She'd never seen her poodle take to anyone so quickly. Her estimation of the dog's better instincts went down a notch. "That's Travis."

He bent down to pet the dog. Travis's tongue coated Scott's hand with wet affection. "Get many repeat burglars?"

Matrice shook her head as she reached for Travis's collar. "He's not usually this friendly. Travis, stop that."

"It's okay." Scott placed his hand over hers to keep Matrice from pulling the animal away. "I always wanted a dog. Never seemed to get around to getting one, though." Kneeling on the floor, Scott scratched the white toy poodle behind the ears and Travis looked as if he had lost his heart to Scott completely.

So much for loyalty, she thought, watching the two of them. She supposed that this display did speak well of Scott. The last couple of dates she had gone out with had requested that Travis be locked up in the kitchen. She had locked them out instead.

"Would you like anything?" Scott raised his eyes toward her face at the question. Something turned over in her stomach while utterly freezing her mental functions as effectively as if they were trapped in the center of a glacier. "To drink," she added haltingly, finally finding her tongue. "Would you like anything to drink?" she repeated, stringing the words together correctly. She was behaving like a fool, she thought. Why did he keep doing that to her? She wasn't like this with anyone else.

He could think of something he'd like, but he couldn't afford to indulge. Things were already too messed up as it was. Travis barked and he turned his attention back to the romping ball of fur. "Coffee, if you have it."

She had put the coffee maker on a timer when she left for the party. The coffee was hot and rich. Just what she needed to keep her awake, Matrice thought, as if having Scott here wasn't enough.

She took out two cups from the cupboard. "Why wouldn't I have it?" she wanted to know. Did he think she was such a poor housekeeper that she couldn't keep coffee on hand?

Matrice poured him a cup. "Just because I don't cook as well as you doesn't mean I'm a lousy housekeeper."

Why did she turn everything into a war? he wondered. "I'm not trying to get into another argument, Matrice, I was just making conversation." Cup in hand, he sat down on the sofa. Travis positioned himself at Scott's feet, completely forsaking Matrice. "You've got to stop attacking everything I say as if it's in code."

"The same could go for you," she retorted defensively. He wasn't simon-pure in this matter. It took two to argue and he did more than his fair share.

Scott took a long sip of his coffee before he answered. His system jolted to attention. "Are we having that big argument that's a prelude to our engagement breakup?"

The grin on his face had her backing off a little. Maybe she *was* getting too worked up, she thought, but he made her feel edgy. Her feelings for him made her feel antsy, as if there was too much caffeine in her body.

She glanced at her watch. "Being on good terms for an hour is probably a record for us."

Her coffee was strong enough to wake the dead. He wondered how much she used per cup. If it was less than three tablespoons, he'd be surprised. "No, it was longer on the island."

She shook her head. She didn't want to think about the island. She had been all too vulnerable while there. And he had witnessed it all. "That's different. It only seemed longer."

He studied her face. A tiny nerve began to throb in her cheek. Did remembering make her nervous? Was that a good sign? He found himself hoping so. "A lot of things seemed different there."

She looked at him suspiciously. Was he making another dig? "Such as?"

He carefully placed the lethal coffee on the table and leaned back. His eyes were on her face. "You." He smiled, lightly touching her cheek. The nerve jumped beneath his fingers. "There were actually moments I found you sweet and desirable."

His voice was entirely too seductive. She struggled against its effects. "Instead of shrewish and repulsive," she countered.

Scott felt his patience being tested to the limit. "You're doing it again. You happen to be right, but you're doing it again. You're reading things into everything I say."

Reading nothing, what other meaning could she possibly get out of his words? "But you do find me shrewish and repulsive."

He sighed, dropping his hand from her face before he was tempted to reach a little farther and choke her. "Shrewish goes without saying. Repulsive?" The look on his face told her what he thought of that assessment. "You have mirrors, don't you?"

She was no longer sure what he was saying. He had called her a shrew, yet she was sitting here, waiting for kind words. Was she crazy? She was beginning to suspect she knew the answer to that and she didn't like it. "Is that a compliment?"

Of course it was a compliment. Why did she need a road map? He let out a short sigh. "That's an observation. Do what you want with it."

Matrice looked at the contented dog at his feet. Everything was rebelling against her: her dog, her mother, even her own common sense. God knows her body had abandoned ship a long time ago and was siding with him. "Maybe I can train Travis to be an attack dog." She turned to face Scott. "Want to be the training dummy?"

The last word was said with gusto. "Is that a crack about my intelligence?"

She laced her fingers together over her knee and smiled. "Now who's reading things into words?"

She was right; he was doing exactly what he was accusing her of doing. He raised his hands in mock surrender. "Truce?"

She was never ready to accept anything at face value with him. "Depends how long."

For once that sounded like a fair enough condition. "Long enough for us to discuss what we're really going to do."

She shrugged. It seemed simple enough, she supposed. On the surface, at least. Nothing seemed simple once you got past that level anymore. "Tell everyone that it was a mistake, like we told my mother and your sister-in-law." She looked up at him. "It is a mistake, you know. It would never work out between us." She wasn't entirely certain whether she was attempting to convince him or herself.

He began to lazily stroke his fingers along her cheek again, like a sculptor feeling for the image he knew in his heart was trapped somewhere within a perfect square of marble, just waiting to be released. "Nope, not a chance."

She was having difficulty breathing, she realized. He was making her lungs constrict at the same time that her pulse rate was increasing. "We have nothing in common besides education and careers."

He raised her hair and pressed just the slightest kiss to the side of her neck. "There's baseball."

Hot. The room was definitely getting hot. Maybe the air-conditioning system was failing. Maybe she was. "We root for opposite teams."

What was it about this woman that made him want her so? That made him forsake common sense and want nothing else but to be with her forever. He knew what a disaster that would be. Yet he wanted it with his whole heart and soul. "Don't forget Laurel and Hardy."

Who? Oh, yes, the comedy team. She struggled to think. "Who's your favorite?"

It took him a minute to clear his head. The scent on her throat had pushed everything else out. "Hardy."

She shivered as the kisses grew longer, making her melt. "Figures. I like Laurel."

He took her face in his hands, his eyes holding her prisoner. "See, it's hopeless. It would never work."

She could barely breathe as she agreed. "Not in a million years."

Lightly he brushed his mouth against hers, teasing her. Torturing himself. He sat back to catch his own errant breath. "Funny thing though, how everyone seems to be conspiring to get us married. First our families, then our friends."

Funny? No, there wasn't anything funny about it. If it hadn't been for them, she wouldn't be feeling like this. Adrift, lost, confused. And so full of longings and desires, she thought she would explode.

"Misunderstandings," she clarified, because she didn't want him suspecting how she really felt. It didn't seem to be bothering him. She, however, was losing her edge.

"Absolutely."

She wanted to shove him, to hurt him. "You're being too agreeable."

He grinned. "Sorry, lost my head. Would you mind saying something annoying now?"

It was an odd request. "Why?"

"Because if you don't, I'm going to kiss you."

"Kiss me? What do you call what you've just been doing?" she demanded.

"Warming up." He pulled her onto his lap before she could say anything further and ruin the moment they both wanted to happen.

Burying his hands in her hair, he pulled her closer to him until their lips met. The kiss was slow, languid, taking a moment to ignite. When it did, Matrice felt as if she was standing before a huge autumn bonfire with multicolored leaves swirling about in the flames before giving up the ghost and succumbing to the inevitable.

Her body molded against his and she laced her arms around his neck. It was ludicrous, but she felt safe here, safe in the haven of his arms. Safe anywhere as long as he held her like this and kissed her so that the world sank into a black hole, leaving only the two of them.

His mouth slanted over hers as he feasted on a meal that was constantly being replenished, like the old fable about the pitcher of milk that never emptied no matter how many glasses it poured. She was like that for him. The more he took, the more there was.

And the more he wanted.

But she didn't want this. She had told him as much, with every word, with every movement. He couldn't force himself on her, couldn't take advantage of the weakness of the moment, even though she seemed to be willing. *Seemed* wasn't good enough. He had to be sure. And he wasn't. That was the rub. He wasn't. Not of her.

Exercising more restraint than he thought himself capable of, Scott took hold of her shoulders and moved Matrice away from him. She looked at him with eyes that were dazed and confused. And then bereft.

He pressed his lips together, summoning willpower that was quickly deserting him. "I'd better go before we consummate the engagement." Easing her from his lap, he rose. The look he gave her was regretful. "It'd be too hard to get the annulment then."

She nodded, following him to the door. "See you around," she murmured, holding on to the door with hands that were shaky.

" 'Here's looking at you, kid.' "

"Bogart to Bergman, *Casablanca*. 1942," she answered mechanically.

"Kid stuff. Tomorrow's quiz will be harder. Study." He moved to kiss her again, then stopped himself. With a nod, he left.

He was making sense. Matrice dragged her hand through her hair. God, how she suddenly hated sense. Most of all, she hated this feeling of being incomplete when he wasn't in the room.

She looked down at the dog who was pawing at the closed door and whining. "Me, too," she murmured. She leaned against the door, suddenly exhausted. "Travis, I'm coming unglued."

Maybe it was her, but when the dog barked, he sounded as if he agreed.

Scott tried. The entire weekend, he tried.

It was no use.

He decided that the only way he could erase Matrice from his mind was to submit to a lobotomy. Nothing short of that would work. Otherwise, the more he resisted, the deeper he sank. He had wandered unknowingly into a pool of quicksand and trying to fight his way out only made it that much worse for him.

He was going under for the last time.

Desperate, he even went so far as the draw up a chart with pros and cons and then crumpled up the paper. It seemed like a completely lifeless, emotionless way to approach his problem, and he was neither emotionless or lifeless. Especially not when it came to Matrice. Because of her, his emotions were completely turned inside out. What worried him most was that he couldn't dissect the situation the way he usually could or make any sense out of it. She drove him crazy, argued with everything he said, had completely opposite views on every single topic they discussed.

And yet he felt incomplete unless he was with her. It didn't make any sense.

"It's not supposed to make sense, Scottie," Valerie told him that Sunday when he confided in her after brunch. "Love never does."

Scott looked at Val in horror as he helped her clear the dishes from the table. He followed her into the kitchen, finally finding his tongue.

"I am not in love." He thought of it in terms she could relate to. "Love is wanting to sing in the rain, to throw coins in some fountain in Italy and crow with shampoo in your hair while dancing on an island."

Valerie laughed as he deftly cited key scenes in *Singin' in the Rain, Three Coins in the Fountain* and *South Pacific*. She placed the dishes into the dishwasher. "You've been watching too many old movies."

"Those were from all the old features you used to drag me to." He smiled fondly. Life had been a lot simpler in those days.

She grinned, remembering. "I had to. Frank hated them."

Some of his best memories involved watching corny movies with Valerie. That is, until he had gotten stranded on the island—in more ways than one. "Well, anyway, love isn't supposed to make you feel miserable all over," he pointed out. "It's not supposed to feel like the flu."

She touched her lips to his forehead lightly, knowing ahead of time that it was cool. It was a motherly gesture, meant to comfort. "You don't have the flu, Scottie. But I do think you're in love with her." He scowled at her and she bit back a laugh. "You know that old line, 'the lady doth protest too much.'"

He leaned a hip against the counter. In the background, he could hear the baseball game Frank was watching with his sons. The sound of childish voices raised in a cheer told him their side was winning. He thought of Friday night and tried not to. "That was about a murder and if you want me to admit to wanting to murder Mary Therese Crusoe, fine, that I can and will do. But I can't agree to your prognosis that I'm in love with her."

Valerie reached for the dishwashing detergent and poured yellow crystals into the receptacle. "You don't have to agree." She closed the dishwasher door and set the controls. "I can see it in your eyes."

He waved a hand at her. "That's desperation."

Now she did laugh. Valerie patted his cheek the way a mother would with a stubborn child. "Same thing."

He crossed his arms. "I'm not going to get any satisfaction talking to you, am I?"

"Not a wit." She cleaned the counter and took off her apron. "Won't change anything, though." She stopped just before walking into the living room to look at him over her shoulder. "Why don't the two of you just sit down and talk it out?"

"That sounds suspiciously like a peace treaty negotiation."

Now he was getting the idea. "The best marriages have them."

He sighed as he entered the living room behind her. Frank and two lively boys who looked like perfect hybrids of their parents were sprawled out on the floor before the large television set. Valerie took a seat on the sofa. Scott propped himself up on the floor next to his youngest nephew. He looked at Val. "You're not going to let go of this insane idea that we're right for each other, are you?"

The boys shushed them, so Valerie leaned forward as she lowered her voice. "I would if I thought differently."

Scott leaned against the recliner as he stared ahead thoughtfully. His mind wasn't on the game.

Brunch had been a disaster. Nothing tasted right anymore. Matrice had picked at her food, aware that her mother watched every movement. Knowingly. The ensuing discussion told her as much.

Matrice put up with it as long as she could. "Mother, I'm not going to marry him to make you happy."

Rita laced her fingers delicately together and studied her daughter across the table. "I'm not asking you to marry him to make me happy. I'm asking you to marry him to make *you* happy."

Happiness wasn't derived from being belittled. "Mother, the man can't stand me."

Rita raised a brow. "Did he tell you that?"

Matrice threw up her hands in exasperation. "Everything he does tells me that."

Rita was unconvinced. She probed further. "Has he kissed you?"

Matrice sighed, staring at her basically untouched meal. Her entire attempt at brunch was to make patterns in the syrup on her waffles. "Yes."

The look on her daughter's face told her volumes. "More than once?"

She wanted to lie. She knew that she couldn't. "Well, yes, but—"

Rita wanted to clap her hands together, but restrained herself. She knew it! "He must really hate you, then."

Matrice pushed her chair back and rose, frustrated. Her mother was supposed to be on her side, not championing the opposition. "Mother, you're not seeing this in the right light."

Rita turned so she could watch Matrice as she paced the length of the room. Sun streaming in from the terrace highlighted her movements.

"I'm trying, dear, I'm trying." She took a sip of her tea as she thought the matter over. "Now, he's a Harvard graduate, intelligent, hardworking, with a successful career in the same field that you excel in. You both like baseball, concerts and theater in the round—yes, I've done my homework," she said in answer to the surprised look on Matrice's face.

"You're the same nationality, the same religion, about the same age," Rita continued. "You're young, vibrant and, as far as I know, you've both had all your inoculations. I need a little help here. Just where *is* the difficulty, dear?"

"The difficulty is—" Matrice swung around and crossed to her mother. She leaned over, her hands on the chair bracketing Rita. "The difficulty is he picks apart everything I say."

Rita nodded sagely. "And you just meekly stand there and take it."

"No, of course not."

With the face of a newborn, innocent babe, Rita asked, "What do you do?"

"I—" Matrice stopped and looked knowingly at her mother. "I know where you're taking this, Mother, but it won't work. I don't argue with him, I just defend myself."

"That might be the way he sees it, too, when he's 'not arguing' with you." Rita covered Matrice's hand with her own. "Why don't you stop running from commitment and give this another try?"

Matrice pulled back her hand and started to pace again. "I'm not running from commitment."

Rita knew better. "Oh, yes you are. You're my daughter and I know you better than you think. Commitment's a very scary concept, promising to love just one man forever." She nodded, remembering. "I know, I felt it, too."

"You?" Matrice stopped pacing and drew closer again. "But Dad was so terrific."

"I know. But that has nothing to do with it," Rita said mildly. "It's still a very frightening thing to come to terms with and men don't have an exclusive corner on that sort of fear. I think that might be what's coloring your judgment. You're trying too hard to find things wrong with him. And still failing."

"Failing?" Matrice fairly hooted. "Would you like to see a list?"

"All I care about is the bottom line and I can see that in your eyes when you talk about him. Now are you going to call him and get together or not?"

Matrice sank into her chair. For some mysterious reason, a portion of her appetite had returned. "If I say no, you'll probably find a way to maroon us on another island."

Rita smiled. "If that's the only way..." She let her voice trail off.

Matrice sliced her knife into the waffle, remembering the taste of the fish he had grilled. Fish that she had caught. A balance, that's what it had been. While they had been on the island, they had managed to work together. "I suppose it can't hurt."

Victory. Rita wondered how long it would take to print up wedding invitations. This was a relationship that was going places in a hurry. And soon.

"The only thing that hurts, daughter of mine, is loneliness, especially without any memories." Rita reached over and gave Matrice's hand a reassuring squeeze. "Make some memories, darling, before you lose the chance."

Chapter Ten

Scott decided to go about the matter as if it was a project, a brand-new stock on the market to research. He needed input. The most readily available was word of mouth. He called people he knew within the Wall Street community and asked, discreetly when it was possible, outright when it wasn't, what they knew about Matrice.

Or, if they didn't know her personally, if they knew someone who *was* acquainted with her. He hoped, as he spent his lunch hours tapping out numbers on the telephone pad, to find something concrete to help bring him to his senses. Some skeleton in her closet, an ex-lover who labeled her a veritable Tartar, something.

Anything.

Like a man going down for the third time, Scott was clutching at anything that drifted by, hoping it would keep him from drowning.

He was beginning to believe he was doomed, he thought, as he tapped out the last number on his list of friends.

What he had found, after a week of intense digging, was a great deal to admire. Matrice was an honest, intelligent woman who had attained her position in the firm through almost nonstop hard work rather than through double-dealing. Her social life had been healthy, but not excessive and had petered out in the last year as her work took over the brunt of her time. She had never, apparently, gotten serious with anyone.

He might as well have been putting together a file on himself. Everything he learned was mirrored in his own life.

If he wanted something to help free him of this emotional quandary he was in, he hadn't found it. The more he delved, the more he discovered that he and Matrice had a myriad of things in common. No wonder Valerie had been so certain, he mused.

He cradled the phone against his shoulder and made himself comfortable in the chair as the line on the other end was picked up. "Hello?"

"Hank? Scott diMarco. I was wondering, what can you tell me about Mary Therese Crusoe. I was just—"

He got no further as the stockbroker he had interned with laughed. "Hey, what is it with you two? Are you filling out questionnaires on each other?"

Scott sat up and took the receiver into his hand. He placed a check mark next to Hank's name. Maybe this was finally something. "What do you mean?"

"Well, she called me yesterday to ask about you and now you're calling to ask about her. I thought you two were engaged. Or is that just a vicious rumor?"

Scott wasn't certain if it was his imagination, or if that was a hopeful note he detected in Hank's last question. "Um, yeah, we are." They were going to have to do something about correcting that, he thought. He began to doodle impatiently. "About Matrice—"

The man cut him off again with the expertise of a New York cabdriver jockeying for position on the 59th Street Bridge. "Well, why don't you talk to each other for God's sake instead of pussyfooting around?"

There was a pause and Scott started to speak, but he wasn't quick enough.

"Are you looking for dirt on her?"

Scott didn't want to call it that—ammunition was more like it. "Just being curious." He sounded about as convincing, he thought ruefully, as Pinocchio with his nose stretched out two feet in front of him. "Look, I—"

Hank continued as if Scott hadn't even tried to answer him. "Because if you are, you won't find any."

Scott had no idea why he was grinning. This was his fate he was attempting to save. Wasn't it? "I'm beginning to realize that."

"What surprises me—" the deep voice vibrated against Scott's ear "—is that she said yes to you."

He and Hank had gone to Harvard together and had started out at the same firm straight out of college. He'd never been crazy about the man, Scott decided. "Thanks a lot."

"No, I mean it. You're a great guy and all that, but hey, it's not like you're made out of gold or anything."

It almost sounded as if Hank was licking his wounds. Had he been involved with Matrice? Scott gripped his pencil tighter as he doodled. "Just what is it you're trying to say?"

"I know a couple of guys who would've liked to try waltzing down that aisle with Matrice. Including yours truly. No go." Scott heard Hank sigh wistfully. "She's a fun date as long as everything stays nice and loose. The only commitment she seems to have ever made is to her work and that dust mop of hers that she calls a dog. I know she froze me out as soon as I started getting serious."

Scott glanced down at the paper on his desk and stared. As he sat, listening to Hank, his doodles had deteriorated into tiny hearts. Linked hearts. Scott stopped doodling.

"Hey, are you still there?" Hank demanded.

He realized he had drifted off. "Yes, I'm still here." He wadded up his list of names and tossed it into the trash can next to his desk. "Thanks, Hank, you've been a great help."

"No problem. But I get another crack at her if it doesn't work out between you two."

Scott smiled. "I wouldn't hold my breath if I were you, Hank." He hung up and laced his fingers behind his neck, rocking in his chair.

So, she was checking him out, was she? He might have found that insulting if he hadn't been doing the very same thing and understood the motivation behind it.

Turning his chair, he looked out on the skyline. Usually, it was murky gray around this hour. Today, it was a crystal blue. Blue, just like the water had been that first afternoon they'd spent on the island. He could feel his body humming as the scene materialized in his mind.

No, no more reruns for him. He was ready, he decided, for some brand-new episodes.

He picked up a file from the corner of his desk. He had been looking for something earlier this week and had discovered the file on Rodell Marlow wedged between his desk and his drawer. It was a file he had put together with a few personal annotations. The man's likes, dislikes, things that would place him on a more personal basis with Marlow. He hadn't had a chance to use it. Scott was going to toss it away when something had stopped him. Now he smiled at it. The file would give him a perfect excuse to call Matrice again. Once they got together, he'd take it from there.

And he intended to take it rather than have it take him, the way the situation had been doing for the past two weeks. No more coasting, he was taking over the helm.

They were going to settle things once and for all. There was heat, there was fire and there had to be a reason. If it was the right one, the way Valerie kept insisting, then he was a fool to let a few petty differences get in his way.

Like her mouth.

Scott grinned and shook his head. How could anything that tasted so sweet move that fast and utter so many contrary things?

He thumbed through the Marlow file and murmured under his breath, "'Mistress Mary quite contrary, how does your garden grow?'" He let the file drop on the desk, content with the plans he was making. "I think we're about to find out."

"You all right, Scott?"

Scott swung around to find Jerry standing in the office, looking at him as if he had just lost his mind. He would have felt a little foolish, being discovered mumbling a nursery rhyme to himself, if he didn't feel so damn good suddenly.

"Never better," he assured his friend.

"If you say so." It was clear by Jerry's expression that he wasn't convinced. "I just came by to find out if you're going to be working through lunch again, or if you want to come out and grab a bite with me."

"Sure. My project's resolved." He rose. "I may never work through lunch again." He slapped Jerry on the back and took his jacket from the coatrack. Shrugging into it, he gestured Jerry out of his office. "Lunch is on me."

"What are we celebrating?"

"The right answers," Scott told him.

* * *

"Looks crowded," Jerry observed as they entered Stephen's fifteen minutes later. "Think we'll get a table?"

Scott looked around. "There's a couple over there." He pointed toward them.

And then he saw her. She was sitting at a table for six. There were five men surrounding her. Her head was inclined and she was apparently listening to the dark-haired man on her left. Scott took an instant dislike to him. She was laughing at something the man had just said to her.

Something dark and volatile and utterly foreign to Scott took hold.

Jerry saw the change in Scott's expression and looked to see what had caught Scott's attention. "Hey, isn't that your fiancée?"

"Yes, yes it is." *But who is that jerk next to her?*

The maitre d', a short, heavy-boned man in a dark suit who bore a striking resemblance to a penguin, appeared to seat them. Scott waved Jerry to the dining room.

"You go on ahead, Jerry. I'll join you in a minute." his promise hanging in the air, Scott was already making his way toward the table in the center of the room.

Coming up behind Matrice, Scott placed his hands on the back of her chair, bent down and brushed a kiss on her cheek. Caught completely by surprise, Matrice knocked over her glass of water. It cascaded into her lap like a miniature waterfall. She swung around, ready, with a hail of well-seasoned words to pepper whoever had snuck up behind her. Her eyes grew huge.

"You."

He had never heard one word packed with so much explosive emotion in his life. It was meant to cut him off at the knees and have him crawling away under the table to either heal or die. He knew what her choice would be at this moment.

Matrice grabbed her napkin and began dabbing at the mess on the table in front of her and at her suit. How dare he just appear like this out of nowhere. She had waited for an entire week for him to call her. He never did. Not once. Her answering machine was filled with other voices, not his. There wasn't even a hang-up to allow her to pretend that he had attempted to call. And now he was here, kissing her in front of her boss? Just who the hell did he think he was to waltz in and out of her life like Fred Astaire changing partners in a succession of musicals?

"Matrice, I need to talk to you." Scott looked at the men in her party. None looked too enthused at his presence. He summoned his best stockbroker smile. "Will you excuse us? I'd like a word with my fiancée."

"I'll be right back," she promised, tossing down her soaked napkin onto her empty plate. *Right after I vivisect this man.*

She rose and took hold of Scott's arm, practically shoving him to the far side of the room. The grip she had on his arm was one that threatened to have her nails cutting through his jacket and shredding his skin at any moment.

"What the hell was all that about?" she hissed. "You are not my fiancé, and what do you mean by barging in like that? I thought you never ate in restaurants unless it was business."

There was fire in her eyes. She looked, he thought, magnificent. "Jerry and I are celebrating."

She just bet they were. Probably plotting some sort of a conquest. Or maybe a takeover. Like taking over her clients. She glanced over her shoulder. Was he trying to steal her clients from her by making her look like an idiot? Was he still trying to get even for the fact that Marlow had thrown his firm over for hers?

"I don't care what you're doing," she insisted, "I just don't want you doing it around me."

He saw the dark-haired man watching them and felt another ripple of jealousy before he could smother it. Scott nodded toward the table. "Intimate get-together?"

"In a restaurant that seats two hundred?" She stared at him. The man had lost his mind. "Yes, I'm planning to take them all on, one at a time." She suppressed the urge to slap the flat of her hand against him, but it wasn't easy. "Are you crazy? Those are clients and you just humiliated me in front of my boss."

"I'm sorry." Jealousy, that was what had come over him. Pure, unrefined jealousy. He'd never experienced it before. With luck, he'd never experience it again. "I just saw you with that man and I got—"

Intrigued, her anger subsided for a moment. "Yes?" she coaxed.

This wasn't the time or the place to make a confession. "—a folder for you."

"You 'got a folder' for me," she repeated skeptically. "Your English is deteriorating."

And that wasn't the only thing, he thought, feeling like a complete idiot. Worse, he was acting like one. He was in this deep. "It's a file on Rodell Marlow. A few personal entries. I thought you might want it."

He was being too nice again. She didn't trust him. "All right," she said slowly. Matrice saw her boss looking her way and he wasn't smiling. "I have to get back." She was already edging away.

He grabbed her hand. "I'll meet you here after work with the folder."

Matrice's first inclination was to decline. But it looked as if the only way she was going to get her hand back was to agree. "All right. Six."

"My lucky number." He let her hand go, aware that they were quickly becoming the center of attention. "Now get back to your client before he gets cold."

* * *

It was six-thirty and she still hadn't arrived at the restaurant.

Déjà vu, Scott thought, absently stirring the Scotch on the rocks sitting in front of him with a swizzle stick. There were no tiny clinking sounds emanating as the stick cut through the liquid. The drink had long since gone from Scotch on the rocks to Scotch in a puddle. He hadn't taken a single sip.

Being kept waiting fed on his annoyance like an accordion slowly filling up with air before its release. He hated waiting, absolutely hated it. Scott threw down the pink stick on the table. Maybe he'd been wrong about this whole thing after all. And been right to start with. He'd mail her this file and work at getting his life back into order.

He had already picked up the file and started to rise when the scent of her perfume approached his table two steps before she did.

He turned in time to see her glide by and slide into the chair opposite him, a ball player making it into home plate a second before he could be tagged out. Scott frowned as he took his first sip of Scotch. "You're late."

Déjà vu, she thought. "And you're as charming as ever," she responded brightly with a wide smile she didn't feel. "It couldn't be helped." She dropped her briefcase on the floor beside her. "I was stuck in a meeting that ran over." She looked at the envelope next to his glass. "Is that the file?"

She certainly was abrupt, he thought. But then, he supposed he had been, too. Now that she was here, he forced himself to relax.

"Yes." She reached for it, but he placed his hand over hers, stopping her. "Dinner?" he asked.

She raised a brow, studying him. She knew how he felt about eating in a restaurant. "Is this strictly a business meeting?"

Would she leave if he said no? He took a chance. "It could be termed as that." He took a breath. "A discussion of a merger."

Was he talking about them? He made it sound so antiseptic. She knew she didn't want that anymore. She wanted the passion she found in his kiss. She wanted romance. She wanted—

Oh, God, she didn't know what she wanted anymore, except for perhaps peace of mind. But that didn't seem as if it was coming anytime in the near future. Matrice resigned herself to her own private purgatory. "I'm listening."

Well, now that he had her here, how was he going to go about getting to the heart of the matter? His hands felt cold, as if his heart had stopped pumping blood and had switched to ice water. Another first for him. "I hear you're asking questions about me."

Matrice flushed. Why had she thought it would never get back to him? She picked at the fold in her napkin. "Well, I um—"

"If you wanted to know something, why didn't you just come to the horse's mouth and ask?"

She hated him for having found out. He'd probably had a good laugh over it with his friends. She could just see him. "Maybe because I felt I was dealing with the horse's other end, instead."

He curbed a retort. Unless she had gotten a sudden allergy attack, that was an embarrassed blush on her face. He decided to do the kind thing and ease her discomfort. "I've been asking questions about you, too."

Her brows hiked up on her forehead like high jumpers suspended in midair. He was delving into her privacy? "You've been what?"

It felt as if she could rupture an eardrum with that voice. "Down, Matrice. I'm not going to get sucked into another argument."

She should have her head examined for coming to see this man. He hadn't called her, he'd called everyone else in town instead. "Well, you have a funny way of showing it."

He didn't have a clue as to why she was so upset. He thought she'd be flattered. "What are you so angry about? You were doing the same thing."

She jerked open the cellophane wrapper on a package of crackers from the bread basket. The crackers flew out like so many doves being released from their cages.

"That's different." Avoiding his eyes, she picked the crackers up and placed them on her plate.

He didn't understand. "Why?"

"Because," she answered doggedly.

"Now that makes a hell of a lot of sense." Scott realized that his voice was rising. They were headed for another argument whether he wanted it or not. And it would settle nothing.

With a sigh, he rose. Taking out his wallet, he tossed a ten on the table next to his watery drink.

"Leaving so soon?" she asked sweetly. Though she kept a smile on her face, she felt a pang because he was going. These ambivalent feelings were going to drive her to distraction very soon.

"Yes." He grasped her firmly by the hand. "And you're leaving with me."

People were staring. She pressed her lips together. "I'm hungry," she said stubbornly.

"I'll feed you." He gave a little tug.

The man was a beast, a complete animal. She grabbed her briefcase as he forcefully escorted her from the table.

The waiter was just arriving to take their order. "Is there some problem?" he asked, eyeing the way Scott was holding Matrice's hand.

"We've decided to make love before the appetizers instead of after," Scott answered, ushering Matrice from the room.

"I'll never be able to show my face there again," she cried as she stumbled after him.

Scott was unfazed. "No loss. Food wasn't very good there anyway."

She yanked at her hand, but he kept it tightly trapped in his own as he handed his parking number to a valet. Matrice counted to ten before she spoke, afraid that the first words would come out in a bloodcurdling scream. The valet had returned with the car before she trusted herself to address Scott in front of witnesses. "There are laws against kidnapping, you know."

"I'll chance it."

"What's next, a duel?" she demanded. "Pistols at ten paces?"

He ushered her into the car, then came around to the driver's side. "Your weapon of choice would probably be tongues at twenty." He gave her a look before starting up the engine. "And you'd undoubtedly win, too."

It was ridiculous to sit here as he drove and listen to this. "If you're going to be insulting, I'd like to get out now."

He shook his head, taking a corner. "Sorry, you're out of luck. I'm kidnapping you, remember? We're going to my apartment."

It wasn't a high-speed chase. Traffic was moderate to heavy and he was moving slow enough for her to open the car door and get out. She weighed her options and stayed where she was.

"And just why am I going to your apartment? You've got the file with you. Hand it to me and I'll leave."

"Dinner, remember?" he reminded her. He was beginning to enjoy himself. "And a discussion."

She crossed her arms in front of her. He had embarrassed her twice in one day, three times if she counted the fact that he had thrown her "investigation" in her face. She'd had all that she could put up with for now. "I have nothing to say to you."

He gave a short laugh. "Matrice, you'd have something to say to me even if there was a gag on your mouth."

Okay, that was it. "I've had enough." She reached for the door handle. If she had to, she'd jump out. Her hand tightened on her briefcase.

The car swerved in the lane as Scott grabbed her hand and pulled it away from the handle. "No, you haven't, you've only had half. We both have. It's about time that stopped."

She hadn't the slightest idea what he was talking about. She sat, seething, until they arrived at his apartment building. He guided the car into the underground parking structure.

"I hate underground parking. It always makes me feel like a mole," she murmured.

She gripped the armrest. Nerves. Nerves were coming awake, stretching as far as they would go. Part of her felt like running, but not from fear of what he would do to her. If she were honest, she knew him to be sweet and gentle beneath that obnoxious facade he enjoyed taunting her with. Her week's investigation had turned up information that qualified him for a senior merit badge as far as character went. If he was the type of man to physically fear, his true colors would have come through while they were alone on the island.

What had come through on the island was a man who could work with her, a man who had given her emotional support during the storm and had gone looking for her when he'd thought she was lost. That wasn't a man to be feared for physical reasons.

What troubled her was a deeper fear, a fear her mother had warned her about. Fear she now silently admitted that she had.

She was afraid of committing, afraid of making the wrong choice. Afraid of giving her heart and, somewhere down the road, receiving ashes in its place.

Her fear rose to a vibrating crescendo as he pulled his car into his parking space. "I don't think I'd better go in, Scott."

Her voice was so subdued, he wondered if she had suddenly become ill. He looked at her. She looked fine. And stubborn. Her chin was up. "Well, you're not going to sit in the car all night."

Maybe she had been too quick to award that merit badge. Her eyes narrowed, eyebrows drawn into a V. "You won't drive me home?"

"Nope." He saw the flash of anger in her eyes and felt relieved. He liked her better this way. Subdued wasn't her style.

"I'll get a cab." She got out, slamming the door in her wake. She managed to take two steps toward the Exit sign before he caught her hand. Matrice turned around and glared. "What are you doing?"

"Friday is taking Ms. Crusoe home with him."

She yelped as he picked her up and threw her over his shoulder, fireman-style. "Put me down, Scott. Put me down this minute."

Instead of obeying, Scott began walking to the elevator at the far end of the structure.

"I said 'put me down'!" She was still clutching her briefcase and it was banging against his back with every step.

He pressed for the elevator. "If I put you down, are you going to leave?"

What she needed, she thought, was a clear shot at his head with the briefcase. *That* would get him to let her go. "You bet your life I am."

He patted her behind as he shifted her weight slightly on his shoulder. "Then I'm afraid this is the way you're going to remain for the next seventeen flights." He stepped into the elevator with her and pressed number seventeen.

She gave up. "All right, all right, all right. Just put me down," she ordered. "I feel like a sack of potatoes."

"No," he contradicted, "you feel a lot nicer than that." Before she could say anything else, Scott grasped her waist and helped her down. Her body slid against his until her feet finally reached the ground. "A hell of a lot nicer than that."

She felt it starting all over again, the fire that she couldn't keep under control, the desire that had been waiting all week to erupt. Why couldn't he leave her in peace? "You're making me crazy."

"The punishment," he told her, firmly holding her hand, "should always fit the crime." As he bent his head to kiss her, the elevator doors parted. They'd reached his floor. He sighed and ran a finger along her lips before he led her out. "You're not off the hook yet," he warned.

She had more than a passing hunch that he was right.

Chapter Eleven

Matrice watched in fascination as Scott moved around a gourmet kitchen that was functional as well as slightly intimidating. There was a spice rack on the wall filled with over two dozen ingredients she had never heard of. Pots of different sizes were strategically hung above the range located in the middle of the kitchen, like a squadron of metal soldiers, polished and at attention, waiting to serve. She felt a little like Alice must have felt after falling through the rabbit hole and discovering that the rabbit spoke an entirely different language than she did.

She ran her finger along the rim of a wok. "Do you use all these things?"

Having breaded and fried the veal, Scott began arranging the pieces in a pan. "Not all at once." Well, at least they'd never fight in the kitchen, he thought as he covered the veal pieces with thin slices of mozzarella cheese and topped them off with his own sauce.

She turned to look at him, annoyed. There he was, belittling her again. "I know not all at once. Just because I can't give Julia Child a run for her money doesn't mean I'm an idiot."

So much for not fighting in the kitchen. Scott sighed. "No one said you were an idiot. Why don't you set the table? The silverware's over there." He indicated a drawer in the cabinet next to the refrigerator. "We can eat in the dining room," he suggested. "Dinner should be ready in fifteen minutes."

Matrice picked out two sets of silverware, then crossed the short distance into the alcove that doubled as a dining room. "You really don't have to go to all this trouble." She set the two places, then returned for the dishes. "You can just give me the folder and I'll go."

He pulled open the crisper drawer in the refrigerator and took out the lettuce and tomatoes. He kept his voice even. "Is that what you want?"

No, that wasn't what she wanted. But she was afraid of what she wanted. "I said it, didn't it?" she asked irritably.

"Take those glasses," he instructed when she hesitated in front of the cabinet. She took down two wineglasses. "You say a lot of things," he continued. "Constantly." He could only rein in his temper so much.

She placed the glasses on the table and swung around to face him across the length of the room. "Well, if my talking bothers you so much, why am I here?"

He tossed the lettuce to her. "Do the salad." He bit off the order.

She caught the lettuce and held it in front of her like a basketball. "Sure I won't mess it up?"

You can get through this, he counseled himself. "Garden salad is hard to mess up. Even for you."

She debated finding a new use for a head of lettuce.

Her face telegraphed what was on her mind and he couldn't help himself. He laughed. The tension ebbed away from him.

"What are you laughing at?" She had never known anyone who could irritate her, who could make her so defensive as quickly and as thoroughly as he could.

"You. Us," he added quickly as she raised the head of lettuce for what looked like a forward pass aimed at his midsection. "I suppose life with you would be one big battlefield." He disarmed her, placing the lettuce on the counter. "I'll shred, you chop. The tomatoes, not me," he advised, pointing toward the counter.

There was a host of knives inserted in a block. She pulled one out and discovered she had chosen something that resembled a saber. She eyed the tomatoes uncertainly.

Scott took the knife from her and exchanged it for one that was a good deal smaller. "Chop it. Don't behead it," he urged.

She concentrated on making the slices equal and keeping the blade away from her thumb as she cut. "What do you mean, life with me?"

He tossed the separated lettuce leaves into a bowl. That done, he took wine from the refrigerator and handed it to her. He finished chopping the tomatoes. The knife sang under his hand, rhythmically hitting the chopping board.

"Could you put that in the dining room?" He indicated the bottle of wine.

Maybe he mistook her for a beast of burden, Matrice thought, placing the bottle on the table.

"If we got married," he finally said, answering her question as he slipped the tomatoes into the salad and drizzled bacon bits over it.

Suddenly without any means of visible support, she sank into the chair closest to her in the tiny dining room. She stared at him in disbelief as he walked in with the salad and proceeded to calmly pour two glasses of pink Chablis. "Who says we're getting married?" she demanded.

Though dinner wasn't on the table yet, he touched his glass to hers, then sampled. The taste paled in comparison to the sweetness he found on her lips. "Everyone," he reminded her.

For a moment, she'd thought he was proposing. She should have known better. She shrugged, trying to be nonchalant. "Oh, that. That's just a charade."

He arched a brow as he looked at her. "Is it?"

She took a long swallow of her wine before answering. "You know it is. You were there. It was your lie."

"Yes, I was...." His voice trailed off with more significance than any words could possibly hold.

The timer went off in the kitchen. Crossing to the oven, he took out the veal Parmesan and removed the pieces from the pan. Arranging them on the serving dish, he brought out the main course.

Matrice remained where she was, glaring at him. Why had he just dropped the conversation where he had? Wasn't he going to say anything else? Was he just going to leave it hanging like that? Leave *her* hanging like that?

Scott lifted the serving platter toward Matrice. "Veal?"

"What? Oh." Clearing her mind, Matrice took a small piece.

The food was excellent, but it was impossible to concentrate on it when the silence that hung between them was so deafening. Unable to take it anymore, she seized the only neutral topic available. "This is very good."

"Thank you." Scott studied her. It was, he decided, up to him to pursue. Some things were still old-fashioned. He had to admit that part of him liked it that way.

If he didn't say something soon, she was going to ask to put on a radio. Like a prisoner of war, waiting to be summoned before the court and charged, she felt herself growing steadily more anxious. She hadn't the slightest idea what to do about it.

"Ask yourself this," Scott proposed after fortifying himself with another sip of wine for courage. For all he knew, Matrice could laugh in his face and walk out of his life permanently. "Why did you play along with this 'charade' when Sullivan made that announcement about our engagement?"

She was wondering when he'd get around to that. Now that he had, she wished he hadn't. "Because I didn't want to be embarrassed," she said quickly.

He had considered that and discarded it when he was analyzing his own motivation. He could just as easily have rectified the mistake as she that night. It was a flimsy excuse that tore apart upon examination like a forgotten cotton blouse left out and bleached by the sun. "Sooner or later, we were going to have to admit it was a lie."

She kept her eyes on the plate, avoiding his. "Not before two hundred or so people."

"Informing them one by one is more painful," he pointed out.

Her head jerked up. "I wasn't thinking clearly, okay?" Her eyes narrowed. She had left herself wide open. "No cracks."

He raised his hands in innocence. "None. But I do have a suggestion."

She looked at him suspiciously. "Which is?"

He used his knife to reinforce his point, abandoning the meal temporarily. "Maybe, just maybe, you didn't deny it because, secretly, you liked the idea." He knew that had ultimately been his reason for perpetuating the misunderstanding.

She should have expected something like that from him. She noticed he didn't say "we," he said "you." If it was one-sided, she wasn't about to admit to her side. "It has to be a deep secret, because I don't know about it."

He leaned back and grinned. The lady *was* protesting too much. "I think you do."

She was developing a head of steam and he was about to be blasted. "And I think you are a chauvinistic, egotistical bas—"

If he didn't stop her, she was going to use every demeaning word she knew. "What we need in order to make this relationship work is to have dialogue."

She dropped her fork, staring at him. Hadn't he been here for the last few minutes? The last few encounters? "I thought that was what we were having." And ultimately, what was causing all the trouble.

"No." He shook his head. "What we're having is sniper fire. We need to have meaningful exchanges, not thoughts started in our heads and ending up on our tongues."

He was accusing her of babbling, or something equally as inflammatory. "What?"

He wondered if her co-workers at the firm knew she was a spitfire. He had a sneaking suspicion that she was his own private hellion. He raised his hands defensively, already knowing that she was taking this the wrong way. "I'm as guilty of it as you."

"How magnanimous of you."

He dug a little deeper for patience. The end result, he promised himself, was going to be worth it. "Matrice, shut that beautiful mouth of yours and listen for a change, instead of grabbing at a piece of what I say and shooting from the hip."

She wanted to tell him what he could do with his theory, but held off. Instead, she exhaled a very angry breath and folded her arms before her. "Go ahead."

He looked at her plate. She'd only half finished the small piece. "You can listen and eat if you like. No sense in your meal getting cold."

As if he thought she could taste anything, she thought. "At least that's a sensible statement. Your cooking is the best thing about you."

She had meant it to sting and it did. "Really?"

"Yes."

For two cents—

He caught hold of himself. It wasn't his veal she had been kissing on the island. Or after the baseball play-offs. Like a fox cornered by the pursuing hounds, she was just trying to put up a fight before giving up. He had her and he knew it. "You actually prefer my cooking to other things about me?"

"Yes." She lifted her chin defiantly. His eyes pinned her, pinned her conscience. She'd never been very good at lying. "No," she admitted angrily. She threw down her napkin and rose. "Look, if this is some complicated way of building your ego, I'm not interested." She turned to leave.

He was quick to block her way. "No, this is a complicated way of getting at the truth." He took hold of her shoulders, but she shrugged him off. "It wouldn't have to be complicated if you just didn't take offense at everything I said."

Why was it always her fault? He was as much to blame. More. "And you don't, right?"

He felt his blood pressure rising. She was the most infuriating woman—

"All right, I already admitted that I was partly at fault." A rueful smile crossed his lips. "I guess we are too much alike."

He's lost her. "We've just been fighting over differences, not similarities. Where have you been?"

It was time to lay himself on the line and play his ace card. "In love."

For a second she thought her mouth would slack open and fall to the ground like some third-rate cartoon character's. "What?"

He smiled. "I'm in love with you."

"You are?" A bevy of emotions suddenly blossomed, but then she grasped control again. She looked at him suspiciously. "Is this a trick?"

He shook his head as he took hold of her arms, trying to anchor her in place. "If it is, then I'm playing it on myself."

She wasn't convinced. "Why do you love me?"

He laughed ruefully. "Because I have a death wish."

She knew it. It *was* a joke. Just a joke at her expense, nothing more. He thought her feelings were a joke. Stifling the urge to give him one swift kick to remember her by, she broke his hold and started for the door.

Scott grabbed her hand and spun her to face him again. His voice softened, matching his expression. "And because you're beautiful, and intelligent and stir my blood the way no other woman ever has."

He ran his hand along her cheek. A man should never fight the inevitable, he thought. It wasted too much energy.

"When Valerie told me she was going to find a woman who matched me in every way, she went a little too far and did her job a little too well. You're just as stubborn as I am, Matrice. More, probably, because I'm the one who's giving in."

"Giving in?" she echoed. What was he talking about?

"I'm asking for a truce."

She could feel the heat of his body, warming hers. "Is that all?"

"I'll ask for more if I know that I'm not standing on quicksand." He looked into her eyes and saw the answer that he needed.

The smile on her lips had its roots in her soul. "The ground was never safer, 'Friday.'"

He threaded his hands around her waist, holding her close. "Does that mean you love me?"

Her throaty laugh went straight to his head the way the wine never could. "What do you think?"

He increased, not sated his hunger with just the briefest taste of her lips. "What I think doesn't matter right now. It's what I hear that does. I need to hear it."

"Your ego, again?" But she was smiling as she asked.

He fitted her body against his. "Don't forget my self-esteem, which has been taking a beating ever since I met you."

She thought of all the things he had said to her. All the things he had inferred. "You deserved it," she informed him. He nipped her lower lip again, making her want. Tantalizing her. "Not," she added breathlessly. "I love you, you know that. It's what drove me so crazy. You knew it all along, ever since the island. And I didn't have a clue about you." She sighed as he kissed her again, this time more deeply. She could live on this alone, she thought. "So what do we do about this?"

He grazed her throat, exciting himself as well as her. "We're both logical people—"

She laughed, though it wasn't easy when her bones were dissolving. "When we're not around each other." Two could play this game, she thought.

"True." He felt himself on shaky ground as she pressed a kiss to his throat. "What's the logical conclusion?" he probed.

She wanted it so bad, she could taste it. But she had thrown so many roadblocks in the way. Maybe he was going to suggest just living together, and that wasn't enough for her. Not with him. She wanted forever. With rice and toasters and a veil. "Marriage?"

He laughed and nodded. "Marriage."

Happiness erupted within her like champagne from a newly uncorked bottle. "When?"

"Soon," he promised. "As soon as possible. I want to start the honeymoon."

So many other men would have tried to get her out of her clothes by now. She realized that she loved him very, very much for this measure of restraint. And for so many other things. She grinned. "You are old-fashioned, aren't you?"

He toyed with a button on her blouse, then let it drop. "Only at times."

She lifted her mouth to his. "I'm glad you chose your time well."

Scott buried his hands in her hair as his lips covered hers. "Very, very well."

He glanced at his watch. Late, he was late. First time in his life and it had to be on his wedding day. Screeching to a halt before St. Patrick's Cathedral, he let out a sigh of relief. There was someone waiting to park his car for him. He tossed the usher his keys and dashed up the multitude of stairs leading to the cathedral.

Breathless, he hurried through the side entrance of the church and made his way to the vestibule reserved for the groom. Valerie and Frank were waiting for him. Frank, his best man, let out an exaggerated sigh of relief.

Valerie, resplendent in a deep forest green dress, looked visibly worried. She embraced Scott as he came through the door.

"What happened, Scottie?" She stepped back to see if anything was wrong. "You're never late. I was beginning to think that you'd changed your mind and weren't coming."

"Traffic," Scott told her, giving her a quick kiss. It had been Matrice's excuse to him that first meeting in the restaurant. Maybe they were destined to become completely alike as time went on, he mused.

Valerie straightened Scott's tie for him and patted down his collar. It made her feel better to fuss, he realized. "I would have made it if I had to be brought in by an ambulance on a stretcher," he assured her and saw a knowing smile lift her lips.

The strains of "The Wedding March" began.

Frank took hold of his arm, urging him toward the altar. "We'd better get out there."

Scott nodded, but stopped to give Val one last kiss on the cheek. "You done good, Val." He squeezed her hand fondly.

Valerie sniffed. She had sworn to herself that she wasn't going to cry, but she could see that it wasn't a promise she was destined to keep. She shooed Scott and her husband out of the room. "Get out here before I ruin my mascara and look like a raccoon."

The photographer snapped one last photograph before easing from the tiny room. His assistants were already setting up to the left of the altar where he would take his next series of shots.

Rita smiled into her daughter's radiant face. A bittersweet pang washed over her. "I wish your father was here to give you away, darling."

The first strains of "The Wedding March" were just beginning. Matrice felt her heart do a little flip-flop. "I do, too." She was going to march down the aisle on the arm of her mother's cousin. The man whose island she had found her happiness on. It seemed appropriate. "I want to thank you, Mother."

Rita fussed with Matrice's veil, though it was picture perfect. She needed something to do with her hands besides clutch tissues. "For what?"

Matrice smiled. "Everything. Especially for not listening to me."

Rita laughed softly. "It's always been my pleasure not to listen to you, Mary Therese." She took Matrice's hands in hers and spread them wide, taking one last long look. Matrice was wearing her wedding dress. She doubted if she had looked half so lovely thirty years ago. "You look beautiful."

"I feel beautiful." There was a soft knock on the door and Matrice pressed a hand to her stomach. Giant knots were being formed inside.

"Are you afraid?" Rita's brow furrowed with a wave of empathy.

"Yes." Matrice picked up her train and started for the door. Scott was waiting for her at the other end of the aisle. "But it's a good kind of fear. I don't want to run away anymore. I want to run toward. I want to discover what there is ahead." She gave her mother a self-deprecating smile. "I'm only afraid that it'll stop."

This was what she had wanted for her daughter all along. Rita hugged Matrice, careful not to crush any of the delicate beadwork on the bodice.

"Don't let it," she told her. "Happiness stays if you hold on to it with both hands and always remember to keep it fresh."

Stepping aside, she opened the door to admit her cousin Gerald.

He had an air about him like that of an old-fashioned country doctor, despite the gray, pin-striped suit. He inclined his head toward Matrice. "Ready?" he presented his arm to her.

Rita handed Matrice the bouquet of roses. Matrice placed her hand on Gerald's arm. "Yes, I'm finally ready," she told him.

They stepped into the hallway. It was time to meet her destiny, she thought as the organ music swelled and filled the church, the destiny that she had attempted so very hard to deny. Thank God it had waited for her until she had come around.

Epilogue

Scott tied the cabin cruiser securely to the dock, which had been completely rebuilt since the storm. He took Matrice's hand and walked from the beach to where the shack had once stood.

It was odd, she thought, experiencing a feeling of homecoming as she walked here. After all, it was just a small piece of land in the ocean. A piece of land two miles square with absolutely no modern conveniences and nothing to speak for it. Still, it was there, this feeling of warmth pervading through her as she looked around. "It looks just the same."

He laughed as he slipped his arm around her. "It's only been two months."

Two months. It felt more like a lifetime had passed since she had first seen the island with her mother. Since she had first been marooned here with Scott. She looked up at him, just the slightest drop of hesitation palpitating through her.

Did he want to be here rather than at some expensive resort?

He saw the concern flicker in her eyes. Was she having doubts? This was where the storm had raged. Where the thunder had frightened her into telling him things she hadn't been ready to say. And where, he realized, he had fallen in love with her. But he didn't want to stay if it made her uncomfortable. "Are you sure you want to stay here instead of a resort?"

She was right. He didn't want to be here. He was doing this for her. She stopped walking and looked up at him. She was ready to return in an instant if he didn't want to stay here. "Don't you?"

"Yes." He grinned as he ran his hand along her shoulders. Even the slightest touch of her skin had him wanting her. It was going to be a very good honeymoon, Scott promised himself. "I have very fond memories of this place."

Such as the way she had looked, swimming in the ocean, with only the waves to cover her. The way her clothes had been plastered to her body when she had stomped into the shack, seething at him. The way she had looked, spear fishing for their dinner.

She remembered his scowl when he had first seen her on the beach. "Yeah, I'll bet. You didn't look so happy when we were here."

The same memory now occurred to him, in reverse. Her shocked surprise when he had walked toward her. "Neither did you."

Matrice opened her mouth and then closed it again. Her grin was almost sheepish. "We're not going to argue, are we?"

"Not for at least a full week." That was the amount of time he thought it would take to intimately get to know every part of her body, every secret place that aroused her.

It would take that long just to lay the groundwork for fantasies that would take him the rest of his life to fulfill. He pulled her close to him again as they resumed walking. "I plan to be much too busy to argue."

"Oh?" Amusement mingled with anticipation curved her lips. And then they stopped as they arrived at the site where the shack had once stood.

They had intended on spending their nights on the cabin cruiser. It appeared that they had a choice now. A small, wooden, prefabricated one-room building stood before them, a new phoenix rising out of the ashes of the old.

Matrice took Scott's hand and rushed to the door. There was a note taped to the door. She pulled it off and read, "Happy Honeymoon. Love, Mother."

"The woman thinks of everything," Scott said with a shake of his head.

Picking Matrice up in his arms, he carried her over the threshold. Inside was a kerosene lantern and a small hibachi standing on a brand-new table. A tiny refrigerator with its own auxiliary generator stood in the corner. A quick examination of its interior showed that it was stocked with food and a bottle of champagne.

"She is incredible," he murmured, impressed.

"See, we're in agreement already." Matrice laughed.

He looked around the small room. "Your mother seems to have done a very thorough job of second-guessing all our needs." He glanced down. He kept the smile from his lips. "How about that?"

Matrice crossed to him. Looking around, she couldn't see anything missing. "What?"

Scott pointed to the single blue roll by the table. "There's still only one sleeping bag."

Matrice turned to face him and lightly touched a fingertip to his lips. "We don't need more than one."

He kissed her finger, then pressed a kiss to her palm. "And each other."

She slipped into his arms as easily as if she had been doing it all her life. "Definitely each other."

He nodded, then sampled one quick taste of her mouth. It was hopeless. He was hooked for life. "See, we do agree on some things."

She sighed, looking forward to what was just ahead. "Just the important ones."

His arms tightened. He was never going to tire of holding her. Never tire of wanting her. "That's all that counts. Hungry?"

She looked at his mouth. "Very," she breathed. She thought of something. "Will you still be my man Friday now that I'm not Ms. Crusoe?"

He shook his head. "Nope."

Now that they were married, she supposed that put an end to that little fantasy. He probably thought it was unmasculine. She knew it was silly, but she had to admit she was a little disappointed.

Scott lifted her chin with the tip of his finger as he looked into her eyes. "I intend to be your man for every day of the week, starting right now."

As she threaded her arms around his neck and molded her body to his, she knew that it was the best offer that she had ever had in her life. And she intended to take it and run.

*   *   *   *   *

**HE'S MORE THAN
A MAN, HE'S
ONE OF OUR**

MAD ABOUT MAGGIE
by Pepper Adams

All at once, Dan Lucas was a father—and a grandfather!
But opening his arms to his grandson didn't guarantee that
he'd find a place in his son's life. And the child's aunt,
Maggie Mayhew, would do anything in her power to keep
Dan out of her family. But could she keep Dan out of her
heart?

Available in October from Silhouette Romance.

Fall in love with our **Fabulous Fathers!**

FF1093

R O M A N C E

Silhouette
R O M A N C E™

THIS SIDE OF HEAVEN

The miracle of love is waiting to be discovered in Duncan,
Oklahoma! Arlene James takes you there in her trilogy,
THIS SIDE OF HEAVEN. Look for Book Two in October!

AN OLD-FASHIONED LOVE

Traci Temple was settling in just fine to small-town life—until she
got involved with Wyatt Gilley and his two rascal sons. Though
Wyatt's love was tempting, it was dangerous. Traci wasn't
willing to play house without wedding vows. But how could she
hope to spend her life with a man who swore never to
marry again?

Available in October, only from Silhouette Romance!

Silhouette Books has done it again!

Opening night in October has never been as exciting! Come watch as the curtain rises and romance flourishes when the stars of tomorrow make their debuts today!

Revel in Jodi O'Donnell's STILL SWEET ON HIM—
Silhouette Romance #969
...as Callie Farrell's renovation of the family homestead leads her straight into the arms of teenage crush Drew Barnett!

Tingle with Carol Devine's BEAUTY AND THE BEASTMASTER—
Silhouette Desire #816
...as legal eagle Amanda Tarkington is carried off by wrestler Bram Masterson!

Thrill to Elyn Day's A BED OF ROSES—
Silhouette Special Edition #846
...as Dana Whitaker's body and soul are healed by sexy physical therapist Michael Gordon!

Believe when Kylie Brant's McLAIN'S LAW —
Silhouette Intimate Moments #528
...takes you into detective Connor McLain's life as he falls for psychic—and suspect—Michele Easton!

Catch the classics of tomorrow—*premiering* today—
only from ❦ Silhouette

NORA ROBERTS

Love has a language all its own, and for centuries flowers have symbolized love's finest expression. Discover the language of flowers—and love—in this romantic collection of 48 favorite books by bestselling author Nora Roberts.

Two titles are available every other month at your favorite retail outlet.

In October, look for:

Affaire Royale, Volume #35
Less of a Stranger, Volume #36

In December, look for:

Command Performance, Volume #37
Blithe Images, Volume #38

Collect all 48 titles
and become fluent in

THE LANGUAGE of LOVE

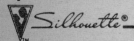
Silhouette®

TAKE A WALK ON THE
DARK SIDE OF LOVE WITH

October is the shivery season, when chill winds blow and
shadows walk the night. Come along with us into a haunting
world where love and danger go hand in hand, where
passions will thrill you and dangers will chill you. Silhouette's
second annual collection from the dark side of love brings
you three perfectly haunting tales from three of our most
bewitching authors:

Kathleen Korbel
Carla Cassidy
Lori Herter

Haunting a store near you this October.

Only from 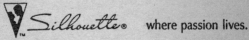 where passion lives.

If you enjoyed this book by

MARIE FERRARELLA,

don't miss these other titles by this popular author!

Silhouette Romance™

#08869	FATHER GOOSE	$2.69	☐
#08920	BABIES ON HIS MIND	$2.69	☐
#08932	THE RIGHT MAN	$2.69	☐
#08947	IN HER OWN BACKYARD	$2.75	☐

Silhouette Special Edition®

#09675	BLESSING IN DISGUISE	$3.25	☐
#09703	SOMEONE TO TALK TO	$3.29	☐
#09767	WORLD'S GREATEST DAD	$3.39	☐
#09832	FAMILY MATTERS	$3.50	☐

Silhouette Intimate Moments®

#07496	HOLDING OUT FOR A HERO	$3.39	☐
#07501	HEROES GREAT AND SMALL	$3.50	☐

TOTAL AMOUNT	$	
POSTAGE & HANDLING	$	
($1.00 for one book, 50¢ for each additional)		
APPLICABLE TAXES*	$	_____
TOTAL PAYABLE	$	_____
(check or money order—please do not send cash)		

To order, complete this form and send it, along with a check or money order for the total above, payable to Silhouette Books, to: **In the U.S.:** 3010 Walden Avenue, P.O. Box 9077, Buffalo, NY 14269-9077; **In Canada:** P.O. Box 636, Fort Erie, Ontario, L2A 5X3.

Name: _____

Address: _____ City: _____

State/Prov.: _____ Zip/Postal Code: _____

*New York residents remit applicable sales taxes.
 Canadian residents remit applicable GST and provincial taxes.

MFBACK3